THE PERFECT BETRAYAL

Copyright © 2021 by Xan Tucker

ACKNOWLEDGEMENTS

THANK YOU to all my family and friends who were so supportive during this writing process. It has been a long time coming. A BIG THANK YOU to all my readers. You continue to amaze me with your unwavering support! I am so thrilled to have new content to share with you all and trust me there is more to come. – Xan Tucker (Your favorite author)

DEDICATION

This urban fiction is dedicated to all the writers and readers of color. This is your reminder to take up your space and tell your stories. Representation matters and regardless to how often people say they are tired of the same stories we all deserve to tell our stories (fictional and non-fictional). The universe has already carved out space for us. It is our responsibility to own that space.

-XAN TUCKER

Alexis Carter

I'm so excited about how things are lining up in my life right now. I'm a new homeowner and finally feel like I've found my grounding. The single life isn't too bad. I get out for fun when I can, but anyone who knows me knows I prefer a quiet night in over a loud club any day. Most nights you can catch me at home reading or writing a romance novel. I guess anything dealing with words makes me happy. This Friday night was a little different though. I was headed out with my girls, Reign and Brooklyn, for some much needed fun. It had been a while. Homeownership was time consuming. It seemed as if it was always something to do.

Tonight, I was going to enjoy whatever Atlanta had to offer and I'm sure it was plenty. First stop of the night was The Spot. The Spot is a fun, laid back nightclub north of Atlanta. It had been a while since I had gone to this particular club and for good reason. I didn't want to risk seeing an old fling, Warner Adams. Warner was my first experience with dating outside of my race. He was fun, lots of fun! We had crazy, explosive chemistry but he was inconsistent and wasn't ready for anything serious. I, on the other hand, was ready for a committed relationship. That was more than a year ago. I cut off all communication with Warner and plenty of other potentials, except one. It was one I just couldn't sever ties with.

I met Reign and Brooklyn at The Spot and it was jam packed. We ordered drinks and food. Reign and Brooklyn took to the dance floor while I sipped my drink. I was definitely just sipping because my alcohol tolerance was so low. I always made a point to eat fries as I drank. It decreased the chances of me getting too drunk, most of the time. I sat watching Reign and Brooklyn on the dance floor teaching moves to the uncoordinated white girl. The waitress brought a round of shots to the table just as Reign and Brooklyn were making their way back. I assumed it was from one of the guys whose attention they had caught, but then the waiter slid me a note on a folded napkin.

I miss you. I know you miss me, too. I knew I would finally see you here. Think of me as you enjoy your favorite shot, Bama Slamma. -Warner

At that very moment, my body defied me. A warm sensation traveled from my neck to the apex of my thighs. The mere thought of the chemistry Warner and I shared was enough to get me within three seconds of an orgasm. I drank the shot and chased it with my Midori Sour. Then I wrote a reply on the opposite side of the napkin.

Absence makes the heart grow fonder. It's not so much of me missing you but you still make juicy jump. She's ready if you are. I'm leaving in thirty minutes. - Lexie

I beckoned for the waiter to come over. I ordered a double shot of Dussè for Warner and had the waiter return the folded napkin. I looked forward to what was sure to be a long night with him. I quickly caught Reign and Brooklyn up on what was happening. Reign found the entire situation to be entertaining. Brooklyn, on the other hand, despised Warner and didn't find the humor in the situation. I just wanted to get laid and I wanted it to be a good lay. It had been more than a year and I knew Warner would be a great lay. We had crazy chemistry. It would be one night and done. I think my whole interaction with Warner put Brooklyn in a somber mood. She was just really disinterested afterwards and while I felt bad, I can't lie like I wasn't excited about getting laid.

Thirty minutes later, I was headed to my car. I felt a small amount of guilt because I hadn't stayed as long as I should have, but my priority was getting laid. I hopped in my car and drove the familiar route to Warner's house. I had driven this route countless times yet tonight it seemed longer than necessary. I'm sure it was pure excitement and impatience making the route seem longer. Either way, I was ready to get there and get the show on the road. Warner may have been inconsistent but his sex game never disappointed. We had done so many unthinkable things together. Sexually, I was in a box until I met him. There was something so liberating about sexual exploration and Warner brought it out of me.

After twenty minutes, I arrived at Warner's but he wasn't home yet. Ugh, where is he? He left the club maybe seven or eight minutes before me. I pulled out my cell phone to give him a call. It was then that I realized my phone was on silent and I had five missed calls from him. I called back but he didn't answer. I waited a few more minutes and called again, still no answer. This went on for about fifteen minutes or so. Finally, I sent him a text.

Alexis: Fuck you and whatever you going through.

So much for my ass getting laid. I drove my horny ass home. To say I was pissed was an understatement. How dare he stand me up! Bastard.

A few days later, I was headed to church for Sunday morning service. Lord knows I needed to hear the word. As I walked out of my door, I made a mental note to call Anderson Lawn Care to cut my grass because my lawn was horrible.

I attended the early morning service which was my preference. The mid-morning service was too crowded. I wasn't particularly fond of being in tight spaces with lots of people. Plus, I enjoyed when the senior pastor preached the word which was likely to happen at the early morning service.

After church, I headed back to my new neighborhood. On the way home, I made the impromptu decision to cook Sunday dinner but I needed groceries. I was lucky that I now had two major grocery stores less than a mile from my house. I stopped at Kroger's with a simple menu in mind: fettuccine alfredo, broccoli, grilled salmon, and salad.

This particular Kroger's was a little different. In my previous neighborhood's Kroger, I had a difficult time finding the seasonings and other ingredients needed to cook the way I wanted. This particular Kroger had all the seasonings and lots of other things as well such as black hair products. While they were a little more expensive, it was convenient to have them in the store. I was still adjusting to having so many black folks in my neighborhood but I think it's going to be beneficial if it meant not having to drive to multiple stores to get what I needed.

I quickly got through the checkout and was on my way home. As fate would have it, while sitting at a red light I saw a truck advertising graphic design service. I was at a point in my new business ventures that I needed to start hiring for services I would need in the very near future. I took a picture and made a mental note to text Slayton's Graphics & More.

Later that evening, I checked off that mental reminder and sent a message to Slayton's Graphics. I needed to stop being so lazy and get to work on my written work as I had promised myself. My first order of business was to get a nice logo but honestly I wanted to get my first book cover done as well. I was ready to publish and see what I could expect next from writing. I sent a short text:

Alexis: Hi, I got your number off the advertisement on your truck. I'm looking to get graphic design work done for a few projects. Do you provide consultations?

Thanks, Alexis.

I received a text message almost instantly.

Thanks for reaching out. Yes, I provide consultations. This can be done in person or via email. Whatever works best for your schedule. I personally prefer in person but again whatever works with your schedule. Thanks, R. Slayton.

Alexis: In person is fine with me. I prefer Mondays as I'm available most of the day. Where is your office located? I'm in South Fulton but can meet you pretty much anywhere in the metro area after 10 AM.

I always made sure I did things after 10 AM to avoid the morning rush hour. I waited patiently for a response.

After 10 AM works for me. Here is the address: 4812 Slayton Drive Union City,GA 30291. If I'm not available, one of my employees will be able to assist you. Thanks and talk to you soon. R. Slayton

Alexis: Got it. Thanks.

Just as I was getting ready to end my night, I received a text message from Warner. I instantly rolled my eyes. What lame ass excuse was he going to give for standing me up?

Warner: I know you're mad Lexie, but it's not what you think it is.

Alexis: No, I'm not mad. I'm pissed the fuck off. You stood me up. That's what it is.

Warner: No, I got pulled over when I made a quick detour to CVS to get some condoms. I was arrested for DWI.

Damn! I didn't expect him to say that. Now, I kind of feel bad.

Alexis: Oh damn. I'm sorry. You're obviously okay. When did you get out of jail? Damn. What happens next?

Warner: I got out earlier this afternoon. Next, I figure out how I can get this shit reduced to just reckless driving. Right now, I would love to see you. Come over, please. And bring condoms.

Alexis: I don't think so. That's an hour plus drive for me and I have to be at work at 6:45. Plus, I think you should really focus on all you have going on right now. It's a lot. Sex should be the furthest thing from your mind.

Warner: But I really want to see you Lexie. I miss you. I know you don't believe that but I miss YOU. Not just the amazing sex. I miss your cuddles. Kisses. Smart ass mouth. You.

Alexis: Warner as tempting as it is it's really not a good idea. Let's try to link up another time.

Warner: Sure. Just kick me when I'm down.

Alexis: Have a good night. I'll check in with you later.

The Introduction

July 24, 2014

It was early Monday and I had already run my fair share of errands. I managed to get a five-mile run in, unpack a few more boxes, and grab a few things from the store. I was now headed to Slayton's Graphics for my consultation. For some odd reason, I felt like I should've dressed up more but it was hot and Georgia heat is no fun. Instead, I wore a black and white sundress with my favorite red sandals. I didn't have on any accessories or my signature lipstick. I really wanted to do the consultation and head back home. It was too hot to be out flouncing around.

I pulled into the driveway of what looked like a really nice house that had been turned into an office space. There were two other cars in the driveway; a black Tahoe and a white BMW. The Tahoe had Howard University license plates and the BMW license plate read, RSLAYX2.

"Hmph, someone is full of themselves," I thought as I walked into the office space. I was slightly mesmerized by how nice it was. The décor was nice and the paint on the walls was very inviting. Lots of light colors complemented with more masculine colors.

I was quickly greeted by a short, dark, muscular built gentlemen in khakis and a polo. I assumed it was R. Slayton.

"Good Morning, you must be Alexis?"

"Good Morning. Yes, I am. You must be R. Slayton."

"No, ma'am. Remington isn't in right now but I'll be able to assist with your consultation. I'm Antonio."

My response was delayed because I was still stuck on the name Remington. Such a cool name. I would love to get to know the why behind it. "Great, nice to meet you, Antonio."

"Follow me into my office and we can get started with your consultation. Hopefully, I can convince you that Slayton's Graphics is your best option."

Antonio was very thorough and if I'm honest, Slayton's Graphics had an extensive portfolio with a lot of great work. I shared my vision with him as it related to my logo. He provided his professional opinion and didn't shy away from telling me when something was too much. The consultation went way longer than fifteen minutes. We talked for more than an hour. I explained to him that I had written a novel series and was finally ready to release it. We discussed book cover ideas after I provided a brief synopsis of each book and the title.

When I left Slayton's Graphics I was more excited about my new venture than I had been in a while. Funny how something as simple as a consultation can change your outlook. I couldn't wait to solidify my logo and plans to move forward. I hoped their work ethic was half as good as the portfolio and consultation.

I decided to treat myself to lunch since I was already out and starving. I drove to East Atlanta Village and enjoyed lunch at LePetit Marche. It was one of my favorite brunch spots in Atlanta. The food was always delicious and it was an added plus that it was black-owned. I particularly loved their Tuna melt, pasta salad, and chips. I dined on the patio and pulled out my notebook to start brainstorming on the announcement of my upcoming novels.

Only my family and close friends knew I was a writer at heart. I couldn't wait to shock the world by releasing my work. The thought of sharing some of my most intimate thoughts made me nervous. Palms sweaty, increased heart rate, and hand trembling nervous. This would be a new level of vulnerability and anyone who knows me knows I struggle for vulnerability. I was ready to let the world see a different side to Alexis Carter. A side rarely shared. At that moment, it dawned on me that I should release a book of poetry first and then release my novels. And so that became the goal. I have at least a hundred poems that I could use in my initial book release. I could barely contain my excitement.

I rushed home and began looking through my poetry. I needed a good way to tie most of the poems together and have it in a format that made sense. Better yet, I wanted it to tell a story. A love story. In particular, I wanted it to tell a love story based on my previous relationship experiences. I wanted people to be able to relate to my writing and the best way to do so was to present it as a love story. Besides, everyone could relate to a good love story.

I was sitting at the dining room table when I heard someone pull into the driveway. Great, I don't need any distractions. I relaxed when I remembered my appointment with Corey Anderson with Anderson Lawn Care. I glanced at the clock and it was just after three o'clock. Why is he here so early? I opened the door just as he was about to knock.

"Hi, Corey. I thought you would be working today."

"Hi, Alexis. No, I'm off. Justice is due to have the twins any day now so I took leave until she delivers."

"Oh, great! How is she? We have to catch up. I'll call her later and schedule time to come visit."

"She's great. Tired and big, but happy. I don't think I've ever seen a pregnant woman as happy as Justice."

"That's awesome! I can't wait to meet the boys. Still no names?"

"No, we can't agree on anything. At this point, they will be Boy 1 and Boy 2."

"I know baby girl is excited to be a big sister soon."

"She is but I don't think she realizes that she'll have to share Justice with two other people. Not sure how that will work out."

"She'll be great when it's time."

"We'll see. She's spoiled rotten and it's all thanks to her mom."

"As she should be. Just knock when you are done and I'll Cash app you. Thanks, Corey."

"Sure thing. Come hang out with us soon."

"Will do. Matter of fact, let me call Justice now."

I headed upstairs to my dysfunctional office space to grab my ringing phone. It was Brooklyn so I answered but made a mental note to call Justice as soon as I got off the phone with Brooklyn.

"Hey, Brookie!"

"Hey, Lexie. What are you up to?"

"Nothing. I was about to call Justice. Corey is here cutting my grass."

"Oh. How is she? Wait, why isn't he at work?"

"Girl, hush. You are too damn nosey but I did ask him the same thing." We both laughed.

"Honey, you are just as nosey if not more."

"Hell, probably more."

"Speaking of being nosey, how was hanging with Warner on Friday?"

"Oh snap. I didn't tell you or Reign. I didn't hang with him. His punk ass got arrested for DWI and never made it to his house Friday. At least that's what he says."

"Wow. Really? When did he get out of jail? Damn."

"He texted yesterday when he got out."

"DWIs are serious, Lexie. I hope he gets it figured out."

"Me too. I'm glad he's okay and no one was hurt. He's always drinking & driving. I hope he's learned his lesson."

"I'm sure he has. Changing subjects. When do you want to plan this housewarming?"

"I don't and I don't want y'all planning it either."

"Come on, Lexie! You have to have a housewarming. It's your first house!"

"I'm not interested in inviting a bunch of folks over to bring me gifts. No. No. And no!"

"Okay, have it your way."

"Brooklyn, I'm serious. No housewarming. I am planning a girls' night out though."

"I said fine. I'll save my party planning for another time. Anyway, I was just checking on you. I will check in later."

"Okay, talk to you later."

Tuesday morning came so damn fast. I stayed up most of Monday night getting my poems together for this new book idea. I was a night owl by nature but adulthood tried to force me to be a morning person. I was not. This morning was especially hard.

As a consultant for government agencies, I usually sat in long, drawn out meetings most of my day. If I wasn't sitting in meetings, I was reviewing antiquated policies and procedures and making suggestions on how government agencies can be more efficient and cost effective with their services. Today was no different. I was sitting in a meeting with a local county reviewing processes and making recommendations.

I was mid-sentence when my phone dinged. Honestly, I was startled because I usually keep it on silent or vibrate. I glanced at the text message and saw it was from Slayton's Graphic. I made a mental note to check it as soon as the meeting was over. I had planned to reach out to Antonio regarding other ideas. Again, all my excitement about my upcoming projects came bubbling to the top.

"Is there a special someone putting that big smile on your face, Alexis?"

"Not at all," I said. "I just had a thought about an upcoming project."

It was uncommon for clients to speak on personal matters, but Danielle and I had been friends since meeting five years ago while we both worked as Field Program Specialists for the state government. We sat in our training class together and quickly became friends. I worked for the state government for several years before becoming a consultant with a local firm. Some days I regret the decision but no days do I ever regret the money I'm making. I wouldn't be a millionaire anytime soon but I made a hell of a lot more than when I was a state employee. I just take the small victories where I can. I thought about starting my own consultant business for both government agencies and nonprofit agencies at some point. I had significant experience in both. While it sounded ideal, my heart wasn't in it and I never finished with the business plan. My heart belonged to writing and mentoring. I just needed a way to bring them both together.

"Back to earth, Alexis."

"Danielle, we can table my personal life until later. Let's continue to discuss these recommendations."

"Sure, but we have to talk later. I feel like I'm missing something."

I rolled my eyes and decided not to address any more of Danielle's comments. An hour or so later, the meeting was over and I headed home to get started on my new project. I made a "Things to Do" list and a list of questions for Antonio. At our last meeting, he hinted that he and Remington had a brand consultant as well. I had questions about if those services would benefit my plan.

The hour and a half commute home literally drained me. Atlanta traffic is unpredictable like that. A twenty-five minute commute can easily triple within a blink of an eye. As soon as I walked through the door, the excitement of my new project gave me the energy that I needed. I sent an email to Antonio inquiring about the brand consultant and updating him on my new project idea. He responded almost immediately.

Antonio referred me to Remington regarding the branding consultant and asked to schedule an appointment regarding the new project. Surprisingly, he gave Saturday mid-morning as an option.

The rest of my week consisted of late nights and early morning. I usually stayed up past midnight working on my new project and I was up by five o'clock to either run or workout. I looked forward to sleeping in Saturday morning but first I had to get through another Friday night with Brooklyn and Reign.

We decided to hit up a few bars on Peter Street. I would see how long I would last. Bar hopping was usually not my thing but I made it my thing this weekend. I had my drink of choice. Now, I was looking for my eye candy of choice. I was in a flirtatious mood and definitely looking for some trouble. I was with the right duo to make it happen. Brooklyn and Reign were the encouragers of all things flirty, classy, and sassy.

It was just before midnight when my phone dinged indicating I had a text message. It was from Slayton Graphics.

Remington: Antonio mentioned you were interested in branding services as well. When you arrive tomorrow, Nicole would like to speak with you for a few moments regarding your branding needs. – R. Slayton

Alexis: Sure thing. I'll see you all tomorrow.

Remington: Look forward to meeting you. Enjoy your night.

I looked up just in time to see a dark-skinned Adonis looking in my direction. There was an awkward exchange of looks for about ten seconds or so. I took in how damn sexy he was. He was about 5'10, dark skin, bald, muscular, bow legged with the most amazing beard. All I could think was, "Who sent you?"

There was something about him that made me feel exposed. Maybe it was the way he looked at me or maybe the way he looked through me. I suddenly felt a chill over my body. I tried to shake it off.

I was brought out of my trance when Brooklyn started talking.

"What do you want to drink besides that tall glass of fine ass man?"

"Girl, I'm sitting here thinking whose son is that?"

"He is definitely checking you out and I know you are ready to flirt."

"You know I am, but I'm going to play it cool tonight."

"Sure, you are...until you get a few drinks in your system."

I looked up and the waiter was bringing a drink and a note to me. The drink was a Georgia Peach – bourbon, lemonade, and peach puree. Not my typical drink but hey, why not?

The note read: **I like your style.**

I sent a note back: **I like your taste. Thanks for the drink.**

He was so mesmerizing, yet I didn't make my move. Honestly, I just wanted to watch him from a distance and he obviously wanted to do the same. I turned my back to him and started talking with Brooklyn and Reign yet I could feel anytime he looked my way. My body would get this odd chill. Each time I involuntarily turned and looked at him. It was something about him that drew me in but I still didn't do my usual flirting. We literally flirted via drinks and napkin notes.

Reluctantly, it was time to leave the bar and I had to leave my eye candy behind. I knew he wouldn't be an easy face to forget. It was probably best that I didn't get his name. I would've been up searching for him on social media sites.

Brooklyn, Reign, and I stopped at a few other places. It was well after two o'clock in the morning and we were starving. We headed to R. Thomas to grab a bite to eat. It was unusually packed but Brooklyn always knows someone and we were seated fairly quickly.

"Lexie, I'm surprised you didn't go into your flirty mode tonight," Brooklyn said.

"I know. I'm not sure why I was holding back."

"He seemed like he was just as into you," Reign said.

"Yea, he was definitely feeling you," Brooklyn said.

"Y'all were doing all that damn elementary note passing and shit," Reign responded.

"I know. He came off as an enigma." My thoughts were lost on the fine ass man I left at the bar without getting a name or number. Ugh. "Hey, it's getting late. I have a meeting in the morning that I need to do more preparation for."

Yea, I have a few things to do early in the morning. I'm convinced Brooke's raggedy ass is the only one sleeping in."

"Much needed sleep. I get the least amount of sleep during the week. Let me be great on the weekends!" Brooke laughed.

I called an Uber as we waited to get back to our cars that were left on Peter Street. The parking at R. Thomas is horrible. My thoughts drifted back to the man at the bar. I can't refer to him as anything other than a man. His whole presence consumed the space and obviously it's consuming my thoughts right now. All this for a man that I most likely won't see again.

Our Uber arrived and we were headed to our cars. I wasn't really engaged in the conversation. I simply blamed it on my alcohol intake. Brooke and Reign know I usually get quiet when I've had too much to drink. I wasn't intoxicated but I needed time to sort through my thoughts and focus on my upcoming meeting with Slayton Graphics and the brand consultant. My thoughts were interrupted by my phone dinging, indicating I had a text. There were only two people who were inconsiderate enough to text me this time of the morning.

The message was from Devontae whom I had saved in my phone as Bum Ass Negro.

Bum Ass Negro: A, I miss you. You can't ignore me forever.

Alexis: How is your child's mom and has she had the baby?

Bum Ass Negro: A, come on. You are overreacting. We were NEVER together.

Alexis: You are such an asshole. Together or not, you have a baby on the way or already here. She's the mother of your child.

Bum Ass Negro: I know A, but I'm telling you that it's not like that with her. And I really miss you. Like really miss you.

Alexis: Look, you are a great person. Even better in bed but you really need to focus on your new baby. Good luck with fatherhood this second time around. I hope it's a girl.

Bum Ass Negro: You're so fucking unfair. I need a second chance...

Alexis: You have had so many chances. I can't give you a thousand second chances.

Bum Ass Negro: Sure you can.

Alexis: Have a good night Devontae.

The nerve of him. Why must I constantly attract fuck boys? I just need a break from people's sons. Dating just isn't for me right now.

After I got to my car, I headed home. I made a stop at McDonald's for a caramel frappe. I was preparing for an even longer night. I had shit I needed to get out of my system. Writing was my therapy when I couldn't run. So, writing and brainstorming it was for the rest of the night.

I dragged my sleep deprived ass out the bed as soon as my alarm went off. It was scorching hot as it always was in late July in Georgia. I decided on some shorts and a cute top with sandals. I thought about something a little more business-like but I just was not in the mood to be all dressed up.

I pulled up to Slayton Graphics and the same two cars as before were in the driveway along with a red BMW. I'm assuming it's Nicole's car. Alright, game face.

I walked into the office and stopped dead in my tracks.

The chocolate god from the bar last night was sitting in the corner office. This cannot be my life right now. The look on his face said he was just as surprised as I was. With his most intriguing smile, he strolled out of his office and headed in my direction. I became so damn nervous. Nerves I hadn't felt in years. I became so aroused by his presence.

"Hi, you must be Alexis Carter."

"Yes, I am. You must be Remington?"

"Yes, I am. So, let's get to my office and chat. Nicole is here and will be ready to meet with you after we are done."

"Okay, great! Let's get started."

"...What do you do?"

"I'm a consultant for government agencies."

"That's not what I'm talking about."

It dawned on me that he was looking at my long ass legs in these little shorts.

"Umm, oh, I'm a runner."

"Really? Like track?"

"No, I run distance. Like half marathons."

"Have you always been athletic?"

"Nah, I started running like three years ago and I've been nonstop ever since."

"I can tell by your legs. Well, really your whole body. You look athletic."

I blushed at Remington's observation. I was the queen of showing off my legs but I felt so exposed by the way Remington was looking at my legs. I also knew he was flirting which I considered to be a dangerous game with me.

"Oh, so I look athletic to you?"

"Hell yeah. I can tell you work out and take care of your body."

"All that from looking at my legs." I winked and gave him a raised brow look while I waited for his response.

"Not just your legs but your arms too. You just look like you exercise regularly and eat healthy."

"Good observation, Remington. So, how did you get into the graphic design business?"

I wanted to change the subject because I couldn't really tolerate Remington looking at me with his bedroom eyes too much longer. He was definitely flirting and one thing about me; I'm going to flirt back.

"Honestly, I'm into a lot of things. Graphic design seems to be the most lucrative at the moment but I believe in multiple streams of income."

"I can definitely understand that. I'm looking to diversify my income as well. Hence me being here ready to embark on a new project."

"Speaking of, let's get started. Antonio shared your email with me. I have a few questions and a few recommendations. Then I can hand you off to Nicole for your branding consultation."

"Great."

Remington asked several questions regarding my desired logo and upcoming project design needs. He recommended that I hold off on logo designing until after I met with Nicole. He was sure I would change a few things after speaking with her. I hope Nicole is half as good as she's being hyped up to be.

I found it difficult to concentrate being in close proximity to him. His scent added to his masculine energy. It was intoxicating in the best possible way. My body was screaming for him. I was warm and tingly all over. It was so weird the way my body responded to him. I needed a breather. Just when I felt like the lust was closing in on me, there was a knock on the door. Remington looked up and smiled.

"Perfect timing, Nicole. I was just about to bring Alexis to your office. Nicole, Alexis. Alexis, Nicole."

"Oh, great." Nicole stuck her hand out and we shook hands. Her handshake wasn't too powerful but I could tell she was about business.

"Nice to meet you, Nicole. I've heard nothing but great things about you."

"Oh really, I'm sure they didn't come from Remington," she laughed.

"Actually from both him and Antonio."

"That's a first. We can head to my makeshift office and discuss your vision, goals, and all that fun stuff."

We headed into Nicole's office. I really didn't understand why she referred to it as a makeshift office because it looked well put together to me. She had at least six monitors set up and what appeared to be all the latest technology. It was pretty impressive.

I discussed my goals with Nicole about not wanting to just build a brand for my writing but wanting to become a household name. When people hear Alexis Carter I wanted them to be reminded of the mogul and not just the author. I wanted an all-encompassing brand attached to my name. I am much more than an author. I'm a creator, coach, mentor, consultant, world traveler, and fashionista. I wanted Alexis Carter to be known for all those things.

"Oh wow! You are doing a lot. You are definitely marketable. However, we need to focus on your initial branding so to speak."

"Great, that sounds like a plan. I'm open to all your creative ideas."

"Initially, I think we should focus on your writing and mentoring. When you are ready to delve into your consulting we will add that to your brand. Creator, world traveler, and fashionista will be easy to incorporate."

"Sounds great to me."

"First, let's discuss your website and what you want that to look like. Once we determine that, we can get you set up to do a photoshoot to capture the image you want. I'm thinking we should focus on fashion, traveling, and coaching. Of course, we have an excellent in-house photographer."

"Of course you do. What don't you have?"

"Remington hasn't left much to be done outside of his brand. We are a one-stop shop."

Nicole and I spent the next two and a half hours talking about my brand and setting follow-up appointments. By the time I left, I was scheduled for a photoshoot the following Saturday, a follow-up with Nicole, and one with Remington.

"This has been very productive and helpful. I literally would not have thought of most of the things you mentioned."

"This is why I'm the brand strategist. I don't want my clients stressing about things I can handle. I will pass my notes along to Remington and Antonio regarding your website and logo. Leave the rest up to me."

"Girl, thank you. I appreciate it. I'll see you next Saturday at the photoshoot. I'll be in touch if I have any more big ideas."

"Yes, honey. Let me know if you do. It was great meeting you and I'm looking forward to building your brand and making you the household name you desire to be."

"I can't wait. Thanks again."

Just as Nicole and I were leaving her office, Remington was headed out of his as well. I'm not sure if it was a coincidence or not but his timing was perfect.

"Are you ladies all done?"

"Yes, we are," Nicole answered.

"Great, I'll walk Alexis out. I'm headed out for a late lunch."

"Cool, see you next week, Alexis."

"Thanks. See you then."

As soon as Remington and I stepped into the driveway, Remington turned to me and said, "I'm about to grab a bite to eat, join me."

"Umm, okay. Send me the address and I can follow you."

"I only have my personal phone so I'll need your phone number."

"Well played, sir," I thought. "Sure."

I gave him my number and he immediately sent me the address to Louisiana Bistreaux Seafood Kitchen. Luckily, I had been a couple times and actually enjoyed the food. I was so damn nervous to grab a bite to eat with Remington. This was all too coincidental.

On the drive to the restaurant, I called Brooke to tell her what was going on.

"Hey, Lexie."

"Hey, Brooke. Guess what?"

"What?"

"You know the guy from last night at the bar?"

"Yes, what about him?"

"How about he's the owner of Slayton Graphics?"

"What? Stop lying!"

"Imagine my face when I strolled in there this morning looking like shit because I didn't get enough sleep last night."

"Bih, stop lying! What did he say when he realized it was you?"

"He was shocked but I was so damn nervous. He's so goddamn fine. He's such a manly man."

"Is that a bad thing?"

"No, it's a great thing but I was literally consumed with thoughts of jumping his bones. And his ass is bowlegged! I'm like Lawd, have mercy."

"It was meant for y'all to meet. So, give me the details. Did you get his number?"

"Kind of. Sort of."

"What the hell does that mean? Did you or did you not?"

"He sent me an address to have a late lunch with him from his personal number so I kind of got his number by default."

"Wait, y'all are headed to a late lunch right now?"

"Yes, girl! I'm so damn nervous."

"Look, calm your ass down and be ready to give me all the details later."

"Of course."

"Oh yea, Reign and I are coming by later so don't be out too damn late with lil dark chocolate."

"Umm, sure you and Reign can come by later. I don't have anything planned. Just in case your ass wanted to ask me that first."

"Girl, please. I will just pop up when I feel like it. See you later. Have fun and don't overdose on chocolate."

"Girl, bye. See y'all around 7:30?"

"Yeah or before."

I just hung up the phone because I literally cannot stand Brooklyn. She thinks she's the boss of everyone, but then again all my friends are bossy.

I pull into the parking lot, sigh loudly, and give myself a little pep talk. I should've used this drive to calm my nerves instead of trying to fill Brooklyn in. Or I could've called Reign. She does a much better job with calming my nerves. Brooklyn is really just a hype man or lil pistol starter as Reign calls her. She encourages all things ratchet yet she is classy.

My thoughts are interrupted by a knock on my window. I looked up to see Remington staring into my car. My breath literally got caught in my throat. There is no reason for anyone to be this damn sexy. My body instantly responded by rising in temperature a degree or two. Oh great, last night I got chills from him looking in my direction and today my body was overheating from being in his presence. I really needed to get myself together. Well, in my defense, he was mesmerizing.

We walked into the restaurant and were promptly escorted to the table. Remington pulled out my chair and I sat down.

"Have you ever been here?"

"Yes."

"Great. So, you know what you like to order then?"

"Yes." He didn't say anything but I realized he was waiting on me to tell him what I wanted to order. "I'll have the honey glazed salmon with green beans and mac and cheese."

"Got it."

"What the hell?" I thought.

The waitress came over and Remington ordered our drinks as well as our entrees. He seemed domineering but I just watched him do what he does. Once he completed the order, he started staring at me. Honestly, I would normally be offended with a man placing my entree order or even just staring at me but I didn't find it offensive or annoying with Remington. I tried to rationalize why I felt this sense of security with him.

"Are you going to just stare or actually say something?"

"I was shocked to see you stroll into the office this morning. I regretted not getting your number last night."

"Oh, really? I pegged you as the type to just pass notes and send drinks all night."

"I was just playing the game with you."

"Oh, it was a game, huh?"

"It's all a game for the most part. In the end, we are both hoping we like each other enough for it not to be a game."

"Oh, really?"

"So, Alexis. Can I call you Lexie?"

"Yes, most of my family and friends call me Lexie anyway."

"Great. Lexie, tell me more about you. Not the fluff stuff. I want to know you."

"Umm, like what do you want to know? I think you have a pretty good idea about who I am."

"No, I know who you want me to know."

"So, you want personal stuff?"

"Yep, all the good stuff that won't be posted on your website."

"Okay, I'm from Tennessee. I'm the baby of three children. I attended FAMU for undergrad and Georgia State University for both of my Masters programs. I love running, cooking, coaching, mentoring, traveling, writing obviously, and reading when I have time. I have seven kids. Not biologically but I claim my nieces and nephews. Umm, that's me in a nutshell."

"I hardly believe that's you in a nutshell but I'm sure I'll get more out of you later. So, you enjoy cooking?"

"Yes."

"But can you cook for real?"

"Yes, I'm a southern woman raised by a southern woman. I can cook for real. I think you've done enough interrogating. Tell me about Remington Slayton, the mogul."

"What do you want to know?"

"Nope, you don't get to be coy. I want to know the stuff not on your website. All the personal stuff."

"Okay. I'm from North Carolina, born and raised. I attended Hampton University. I'm the oldest of three. I have a set of twin daughters. They just turned six. They live in Charlotte with their mom. I enjoy working out, playing basketball, graphic designs, and rehabbing old houses. I also enjoy home cooked meals."

"Oh, really? What are your daughters' names?

"Alivia and Reagan."

"Nice."

The waitress returned with our drinks. I hadn't realized how long she had been away until she returned. I was parched. As I drank my water with lemon, Remington sat staring again. He had to be the rudest person ever.

"You are so rude to just stare."

"You are really gorgeous to me. I would apologize but I don't apologize for doing what I want to do."

"Add arrogant to the list as well."

We spent the rest of our lunch date asking each other questions and learning the basics about each other. I learned that he gets his daughters every other weekend and all summer. He seemed to be extremely close with his family. Unlike my parents, his parents were still married and lived in Raleigh, NC.

The conversation was easy and natural, but I noticed Remington was a natural flirt. I couldn't really complain because I was, too. He was so charming and charismatic that even our waitress was under his spell. Pretty much the same way I was last night and today. It had been hard to focus in his office and it was even harder to focus sitting across from him. Something about the way he looked at me made feel so exposed. All the warning signs to stay clear of Remington were going off in my head. I made a mental note of it but enjoyed the rest of lunch and our conversation.

Remington walked me to the car and asked if we could hang out again sometime. Despite the early warning signs, I said yes. I actually enjoyed the conversation and looked forward to getting to know more about him. He had a weird way of getting me to open up and talk but he shared the bare minimum about himself. Little did I know that was the beginning of our new normal.

I hung out with Brooklyn and Reign later that night and gave them all the details of the day. Reign, who was the most adventurous one, caught us up on all her recent dates and the fun she had been having. I was so incredibly proud of Reign. She had overcome so many obstacles and while it took lots of therapy, she was living her best damn life. She had finally accepted herself and was living in her purpose. Every day she worked hard to achieve her goals and she worked her ass off.

Brooklyn was still healing from a marriage that lasted too long and ended in the worst way possible. I was incredibly proud of her, too. She was healing and having fun while doing it. Brooklyn ended her marriage after seven years when she found out Robert had a whole other family. He had managed to get his side chick pregnant twice, all while my friend struggled with infertility. Although the divorce was two years ago, this is the first time in a long time that Brooklyn has been smiling and really enjoying herself.

The three of us enjoyed a girls' night in, looking at our favorite romance movies and just discussing all the shenanigans in our lives. It was a little after 10 PM when I received a text from Remington.

Remington: Hey, Lexie. How was the rest of your day?

Alexis: Hey you. It was good. How was yours?

Remington: Not bad. Just got the girls to bed after a not so adventurous day.

Alexis: Why didn't you all get out?

Remington: I worked later than I expected so we just chilled at home.

Alexis: How old are you?

Remington: Pippen when he played with Jordan.

I sat puzzled for a moment. Then it dawned on me he meant Pippen's jersey number. I did a quick google search to see what that number was.

Alexis: 33?

Remington: Yes. Did you know or you looked it up?

Alexis: I looked it up of course.

Alexis: Do you send them to daycare during the week?

Remington: Yes. I have them enrolled in summer camp. Every other weekend my sister gets them to stay at her house and hang with her children and I do the same for her.

Alexis: Oh cool. You have a sister that lives in the area?

Remington: Yes, she lives in Henry County.

Alexis: Do you live in South Fulton?

Remington: No, I live in Fayette County but South Fulton was a better option for my clientele.

Alexis: Makes sense. Okay, I'm being rude. Maybe we will talk later this week if you aren't too busy.

Remington: Definitely. Talk to you later.

Alexis: Have a good night.

   The next few days went by quickly.
Remington and I texted or spoke on the
phone daily. He seemed to be more of an
"in your face" kind of guy. After a couple
weeks of phone conversation, I decided to
invite him over for dinner. It was a weekend
that I knew he didn't have the twins. I had
finally gotten a dining room table and could
have company over.
   The dinner menu consisted of lasagna,
corn, and garlic bread. It was my biased
opinion that I made the best three meat, five
cheese, spinach lasagna in Georgia. It was
always on point. Remington thought so as
well. I think he was surprised at my cooking
skills. Remington and I enjoyed dinner and
lots of conversation over a bottle Black
Rosé Moscato. It was great to just have a
good, intellectual conversation.
   A few days after dinner with Remington
we made plans to go out on a real date.
However, the night before our first date I
received news that my cousin had been
killed. I just wasn't in the mood for company
so I cancelled. Funny how life will throw you
a curveball at any moment. Here I was living
my best life and now life as I knew it had
changed significantly. I was sick to my
stomach for days. I was just functioning

chaos. I made the dreaded trip home the
following weekend.

The Return

I finally made it back to Atlanta after attending my cousin's memorial service. Remington called or texted a few times throughout the day while I was away. He was genuinely concerned and it felt good to have someone checking on me.

Upon my return, I quickly learned Remington was unpredictable and that there would never be a dull moment with him. He decided our first date would be to a café downtown that had a live DJ and karaoke. It wasn't my typical crowd but we had a blast. Remington danced and entertained the entire place. It was interesting to see him in a different setting. A few drinks later, we headed back to my side of town; South Atlanta.

It was decision time. Do I stay at his house or does he stay at my house? Either way, we had a decision to make. Honestly, I was debating whether or not I was ready to sleep with him. It was obvious to anyone in the room that we had serious chemistry. Just as much chemistry as Warner and I had. The chemistry wasn't as explosive and volatile as Devontae and I but we had serious chemistry. I wasn't looking for a relationship at the moment. I just needed a consistent lay and lots of fun with no strings attached. Remington had potential to be just that. Shit, why not give it a try? It's not like I had other options. Well, I had options but I just didn't want to explore those options anymore.

Remington brushed his thumb slightly against my arm. "Something has you in deep thought."

"Umm, not really." I was nervous and I'm sure it showed in my voice.

He gently tugged at my hand and my body went on high alert. It became at least ten degrees warmer in the car. "It's fine, Alexis. I feel it, too." I didn't respond but Remington slowly caressed the top of my hand with his thumb. "There's no need for us to rush anything. Let's go at a pace that's comfortable for both of us."

I don't know if it was my imagination or what but it seemed like his palms were sweaty. I wonder if that was a nervous gesture or something else. When I looked up and saw him briefly look my way I knew it was something else. His eyes were telling the story. I wanted to take my eyes off of him but I couldn't. I took in his masculine smell, his dominant features, and his chocolate skin tone. As if he felt me staring, he flashed his drop dead smile and winked. The pool of heat that gathered at the apex of my thighs made me self-conscious. I gripped my thighs closer together.

"That won't make the sensation any less."

I looked up at Remington, horrified. "Oh my goodness."

"It's fine. I'm excited over here, too, but we can go at a much slower pace."

All I could manage to say was, "This is so embarrassing."

We decided to go back to his house. I was pleasantly surprised because he didn't really live like a single man. His house was messy, but wasn't nasty. Definitely could tell he had little people running around somewhere. His decor had a very feminine touch to it. He either had a really good eye for decor or he had a female to help him decorate. Maybe his sister decorated for him? Either way, he had a very nice home. The ambiance in the quaint living room was sexy. It definitely had a get you in the mood kind of ambience. Maybe it was the subtle touches from him or the masculine scent of his cologne, but I got in the mood quickly. Or it could've just been my horny ass. Either way, I made up my mind to indulge with Remington.

Remington and I sat in his living room making small talk but the subtle touches were more than I could handle. I was ready and so was he. I think we both were wondering who would make the first move.

"I think you know what you're doing."

Remington flashed me that flirtatious smile that I enjoyed so much. "I'm not doing anything Alexis."

"Fine, Remington. Two can play your game."

"I'm not into games but I'm not going to pretend like I'm not finding random reasons to make some kind of physical contact with you."

"Why do that when you can just vocalize what you want?"

"Because what I really want to say is so damn freaky and I don't think you are ready for all that talk and action."

"Oh really? You'd be surprised."

Not the one to waste time, I decided to put an end to the flirting game that we were perfecting so well. I leaned in and kissed him. I couldn't tell if he was shocked or just not a good kisser. The kiss was off. We needed to find our rhythm. He pulled back and I gave him a coy look. I wasn't sure what he was thinking but he leaned in for another kiss. We found our rhythm and that kiss was the beginning of something amazing. Not just that night but for months to come.

From that moment on, I was under Remington's spell. He was my Peter Pan and I was his Tinkle Bell. After a few months, I knew my initial wish of no strings attached was out the window. I met his daughters and instantly fell in love with them. They were such happy girls and they looked just like their dad. They were definitely spoiled. They were a lot of fun and surprisingly took to me fairly quickly. Alivia was a handful and very overprotective of her dad to the point that I dreaded interrupting their time together. Reagan was a free spirit and pretty much did her own thing most of the time. The more time I spent around them, the easier it became and I was less weary.

Time moved so quickly. Before long, it was Thanksgiving. It was my first Thanksgiving as a homeowner, so all my folks decided to come visit for the holiday. Remington and his kids were headed to visit his family on the East Coast. I was excited to be with my folks for the holiday, but I knew I was going to miss Remington. I just didn't know how to tell him, so I didn't. That was a long five days. Not that we didn't speak everyday but I was so accustomed to being in his presence that it was difficult. I also knew I needed that time away. To breath. To relax.

Remington was a lot to take in and most days I felt completely lost in his presence. I could feel myself falling for him like I've never fallen for anyone. The time away was a good time for me to pull back. I needed to make sure I didn't lose myself in everything that was Remington. The chemistry we shared would make that really easy to do. I didn't realize how much of my day revolved around him until Thanksgiving. So, I decided I would try to pull back and focus on other things outside of me and Remington. And that's exactly what I did. At least for a little while.

There was only one person who could take my mind off missing Remington and that was my kryptonite, Devontae.

The Release

Against all my good judgement and common sense, I reached out to Devontae. I'm not sure why I made such a stupid decision. Maybe because we always had a good friendship. Good sex and emotions complicated things. I really wanted to know why he wasn't being a better baby father to his pregnant baby mother. I also wanted to make sure he was okay. He really was my friend. I just needed to make sure my horny ass didn't get all in my feelings.

Devontae and I had been playing the game of cat and mouse for years. We both wondered what would have happened had we taken each other seriously in the beginning. Shit, I'm sure we would be married with a child or two now. Hell, I probably would've been the crying, pregnant woman beating on the door to confront her cheating man one night.

The very thought makes me sick to my stomach. I wish he would get the counseling that he needs. He has issues that he needs to work through so he can be an amazing dad. As his friend, I will bring it up to him.

Devontae finally responded to my text.

Devontae: Hi, A. I'm surprised to hear from you.

Alexis: I know. How are you? And don't give me some bullshit information.

Devontae: It hasn't been bad. I have a new baby girl. She's perfect.

Alexis: Congratulations! I know you are excited.

Devontae: Yes, I am and honestly nervous, too. I don't want to fuck this up.

Alexis: You won't. Are you and the mom on good terms again?

Devontae: Yes and no. As long as I do what she wants, we are good. But outside of that no.

Alexis: Give her some time. She will come around or at least y'all can co-parent.

Devontae: Co-parenting is our only option. WE WERE NOT TOGETHER!

Alexis: Okay. Well, aim for co-parenting. How's your family?

Devontae: They are well. They are planning a visit to see the baby.

Alexis: Great. What's her name?

Devontae: Jasmine Nicole

Alexis: Nice name. Well, I was just checking on you. Glad you are well.

Devontae: I miss you. Not on no sexual shit. I miss our conversations and friendship.

Alexis: Me too. I'm always here if you want to talk. I'm still your friend. I'm just not your fuck buddy anymore.

Devontae: A, I need to talk now but I don't like all this texting. I prefer a face to face meetup.

Alexis: We can make that happen. Let's meet in an hour at our regular spot.

Devontae: I'll be there. Don't stand me up.

If I was being honest with myself, I'd be lying if I said I didn't feel a certain way about Devontae and his situation. Sometimes, I wonder when it will be my turn. Damn, let me not think like that. I'll make an appointment with my therapist to discuss these feelings.

I dressed quickly and headed to meet Devontae at our favorite place. It was this nice, quaint bar off the beaten path in Buckhead. It was a real chill place and relatively quiet for a bar. It was one of my favorite places because it was a great place to have conversation without yelling and screaming over the music and other people's conversations.

I was surprised to see Devontae made it before I did. He had to already be seated inside. I saw his gray Camaro parked right outside the bar. I entered and immediately spotted him with his back turned towards the door. That wasn't his usual mode of operation but I promise he must have felt my presence. He turned around and our eyes connected and as much as I didn't want to, I smiled at the boyish grin he wpre on his face. He walked over to me with his bowlegged ass. His grin was infectious. The chemistry was also undeniable. My entire body warmed up so quickly.

"Hi, Alexis."

"Hey you."

We hugged and I avoided his kiss like I avoided my thoughts of Remington.

"So, we aren't greeting each other properly?"

"We are Devontae, which is why we aren't attacking each other like two animals in the wild. We are here to talk."

"Right, let's talk. How have you been?"

"I've been good. Let's talk about you and baby Jasmine. How is dad life?"

"It's actually good." His whole face lit up. The pride in his eyes and the excitement in his voice spoke volumes.

"Great. How old is she now? Give me all the details. You know I have a soft spot for babies."

"She's three months now. She looks a lot like my mom and sister. She has a head full of hair. I usually get her on my off days during the day. We haven't graduated to her staying all night but I'm amazed at how I'm able to handle her by myself."

"Awesome. Look at you out here being a great dad."

"I'm nervous though. I don't want to fuck this up."

"And you won't. You're off to a great start."

"Her mom is so vindictive sometimes. I feel like I'm walking on eggshells."

"She will come around. The situation wasn't ideal for her. How did y'all meet?"

"Alexis, let's not discuss that. It was a mistake."

"So, we can't have these kinds of conversations now?"

"It's not that. It just wasn't an ideal situation."

"Fine, I'll keep that in mind when you start asking me questions."

"I met her out one night. We started fucking off and about three months into it she said she was pregnant."

"So, y'all were fucking without a condom."

"Only once and I know I pulled out."

I laughed. "Your pullout game is weak as fuck then."

"You never said that."

"I never got pregnant either."

"Yea, I know. Life would've been easier if it were you."

"Nah, I would've fucked you up by now. God knew."

"If you say so. She was bugging that night when she came by the house. She spazzed out because I hadn't responded to her calls in a little over a week."

"Why would you treat her like that? She was carrying your child."

"She was also trying to use me. Every other day she had a bill that needed to be paid. Or some other random need."

"Did you get a DNA test?"

"Yes. She's definitely my baby. I really didn't need a test to tell me that."

"Are you going to keep me in suspense? I know you have pictures of her."

"Are you sure?"

"Yes, I'm positive. Let me see your little princess."

As much as I tried to keep the sadness out of my voice, I heard it and I'm sure he did as well. He showed me several pictures of Jasmine. She was absolutely gorgeous. She had a head full of sandy brown hair, light brown eyes, chubby cheeks, and the cutest smile. Clearly, she had her mom's skin complexion. She was a chocolate brown baby.

"Devontae, she is absolutely gorgeous. Y'all did well."

"See, I told you I could make a pretty baby. You didn't trust me," he said and I laughed.

"You did well. I know she is spoiled rotten."

"Not yet but I can't wait to give her the world. No limits for her."

"And she deserves it. She's a special girl to change her dad's womanizing ways."

"I'm not a womanizer. You just don't like to be told anything."

"I'm an adult. I don't need you telling me anything."

"Of course not, A."

"I'm really happy for you, Devontae. Seriously, I know you will be a great dad."

"Thanks, A. That means a lot. You want to be a stepmom?"

"No, I'll never be a stepmom. Maybe a bonus mom."

"I'm single. We can give it a shot."

"No, thank you."

"Ouch. You didn't even think about it."

"Besides, I'm seeing someone. He's a really cool guy so far."

"Really? How long have y'all been dating?"

"I'm not sure but long enough for me to think he's a good guy."

"Do you think I'm a good guy?"

"Of course, just not a good boyfriend for me. You know you have too many options and you like to keep your options open at all times."

"That's not true. Not when it comes to you. If you would just give me a real chance."

"You know I tried that twice and you still were enjoying your freedom too much."

"A, I know. I wasn't ready then."

"So, you're ready now that you have a three-month-old daughter? Hell, for all I know, you and her mom may work things out."

"We won't. It's hard to find someone to live up to your standards. Nice looking. Intelligent. Can hold a conversation. And amazing sex."

"Well, I don't compete where I don't compare and there is no comparison."

"I've been trying to find someone half as good as you are and haven't yet."

"And you won't. I'm unique and everyone you meet will be unique. Maybe you should focus on you and dealing with the underlying issues."

"I don't have underlying issues."

"Really? You do and you know you do. Counseling is not a bad option."

"I don't need counseling. I just need you to give me a real chance."

"We are not doing this tonight. I have tried to give you a chance on two different occasions."

"I WASN'T READY!" He spoke loud enough for the guests at the next table to look in our direction.

"Calm down. You weren't ready then and you are not ready now."

"Whatever, A."

"Look Devontae. I let you hurt my feelings before. I'm not putting myself in that vulnerable situation with you again. Plus, I just told you I was seeing someone."

"Oh right, Mr. Good Guy. Well, why did you hit me up today?"

"Because I'm your friend and I'm genuinely concerned about your crazy ass."

"Right. I don't think your friend will appreciate you hanging out with someone who knows how to fuck you just right."

"You're such an asshole. I don't appreciate hanging out with someone who can be such a jerk. Bye Devontae. Good luck being a dad."

"A, wait. I'm sorry. I didn't mean that."

"But you did. You meant every word of it."

I gathered my purse and headed towards the door. I didn't expect Devontae to follow because he hadn't paid for the tab and he was such a prideful bastard. Oddly, I knew walking out of that bar meant I would never speak to or see him again. I released him. I released the hold he had on me. I was saddened by the turn of events because I really considered him a friend. Somehow, I felt I was doing us both a favor.

The Upgrade

Over the next several months, Remington and I spent a lot of time together. We were together pretty much every night. Mostly at his house which was my preference. On the rare occasion we weren't together, we would spend a significant amount of time on the phone.

Remington was the sweetest. He had this weird way of showing how he felt without saying anything. One of my favorite things that he did was send me YouTube videos of R&B songs that made him think of me. It was apparent that things were getting serious, but I had some reservations. He seemed to be emotionally unavailable at times, but those times never lasted too long.

Remington and I continued with our newfound routine. I would usually only go home after work long enough to grab clothes and check the mail and then I would head back to his house. I'm sure I had created a monster by doing way too much cooking and he did way too much eating. It felt good to have someone to cook for again and it felt even better to be in someone's space. So far, things were going great with me and Remington. We went on fun dates and really enjoyed each other's company.

One of my favorite dates was Six Flags over Georgia. He thought it was a great idea to get me to go out on a random weeknight. It was Fright Fest at Six Flags and I foolishly agreed to his shenanigans. I didn't dare tell him, but I was terrified of roller coaster rides. It was too late to renege on the date once we were in the parking lot.

"Umm, is this a bad time to tell you that I'm terrified of roller coaster rides?"

"Of course it is but that doesn't change that this is our date night, he said. I just rolled my eyes at him. He was a dare devil in the worst kind of way. "Don't worry about anything babe. I got you." He leaned and kissed me on the forehead. This was by far one of my favorite interactions with him. I blushed so damn hard.

"Yeah, sure you do. I better not go flying off these damn rides trying to keep up with your crazy butt."

Remington got out of the truck and headed to the passenger to open my door. He grabbed my hand and brought it up to his lips. "Girl, you are mine. I take care of what's mine. Don't forget that."

"Oh so now I belong to you? Humph, didn't realize I was property."

"Not property but we are linked so you are mine. Now, bring yo' scary ass on." He slapped my butt. Way harder than necessary.

"Ouch. That shit hurt."

"You didn't say that…nevermind…come on and stop whining."

Our first ride was the Goliath. My heart was beating so fast and I was so damn nervous. We were able to skip the line. As we sat in our seats and locked ourselves in, I couldn't help but to look at Remington. He was so calm and I was frantic.

"Hey, calm down. You won't enjoy the ride."

"Easy for you to say, Mr. Thrill Seeker."

Before Remington could respond, we were off and moving. I instantly leaned into his arm. He laughed loudly. "Oh my God, girl. We are just pulling off."

"So, I don't like these thriller rides." My face was buried into his chiseled arm and my heart was pounding.

"Hey, breathe. I can feel your heart beating too fast. Don't think about the ride."

"Really? What do you suggest I think about?"

"Think about all the fun we had last night. I'm sure that scream is a different kind of scream." He winked and kept his eyes on me. I think he enjoyed seeing me blush.

"I'm sure it is."

We rode ride after ride and my heart was in my throat most of the time. I managed to survive all the rides but not without a lot of screaming, cursing, and hanging on to his arm for dear life. Remington got a kick out of that. Although I didn't find it as funny, it was one of my favorite dates with him. I knew then nothing would be average about our relationship if we got to that point. I also realized that Remington was my safe place.

Even with as much time as we spent together, I was still skeptical about how he moved. Some days he seemed off and other days he was on point and very attentive. I just needed more time to figure him out. I also needed my emotions to get in line with my head. Emotionally, I was already attached. My heart and mind were misaligned and it created more confusion than necessary. I just wanted to go with the flow.

Time went by so quickly. I went home for Christmas and Remington stayed in Atlanta. We spoke on the phone and exchanged text messages on Christmas day. I couldn't figure out why he didn't go home with his folks, but I didn't press the issue. He asked if he could go to my house to get something out of the garage. Of course, I agreed.

I found it hard to believe that I had only known him a few months but trusted him more than folks that I had known most of my life. Two years before Remington, I was in a committed relationship with Shelton. On the outside it seemed like it was the perfect relationship, but it dissipated quickly. I wasn't happy. He was just a familiar stranger. I didn't recognize him and he didn't recognize me. I just wanted out but felt obligated since we were actually friends first. Finally, I gave up on the relationship. He just wasn't my person. I was happy to be released from familiarity and pushed into the unknown. Life in Atlanta truly started for me once I got out of my dead-end relationship. I was single and free in metro Atlanta, excited about things to come. To add icing on the cake, I was just promoted at work and my goal of owning my own consulting firm was getting closer and closer.

Fast forward a couple years and now I'm swooning over this dark chocolate, bowlegged, sinfully sexy man; Remington Slayton. He was definitely an upgrade from Shelton, Warner, and Devontae. At least, I hoped he was.

Even with all the romance, I still had work to do. Nicole and I worked together frequently with my branding and marketing. She was really good at her job. We communicated at least once a week and she provided great insight to events that she felt like I needed to attend. We were planning my first book release and she stayed on Remington and Antonio about making sure the website was complete and represented the branding that was desired.

Remington and I kept our personal lives separate from business life. I didn't think it would be easy to do at first but it was really simple. We designated times to talk business and only did so during that time. Anytime outside of that, we didn't discuss business. It worked and it worked well. Life had gotten busy for both of us so it had been a few weeks since we were out on a date. I planned a nice Friday night dinner date at one of our favorite restaurants, Atlanta Fish Market. I made reservations and sent it to him via text.

Alexis: Dinner reservations at 8 PM –
Atlanta Fish Market.

Remington: Okay. Do I need to pick you up
or are we driving separate cars?

Alexis: You can pick me up as long as we
make the reservation time.

Remington was horrible with time
management in his personal life but he had
the shit down to a science in his
professional life. Sometimes, it felt like I
dealt with two different people.

Yet, Remington was on time and I was
pleasantly surprised. We enjoyed dinner
and decided to ride through the city. We
didn't really talk much. We just enjoyed
some soft jazz music while riding through
various neighborhoods. It was well after
midnight when we decided to head back
south.

"Lexie, I brought a bag so I'll stay at your
house tonight. Cool?"

I never stopped gazing out the passenger
window. "Yes, that's fine."

"Are you okay? You're quiet tonight."
Remington grabbed my hand and glanced

in my direction before focusing back on driving.

"Yeah, I'm fine. I was just thinking you were the quiet one." I looked up at him and he was still holding my hand. He brought my hand to his mouth and kissed it. The kiss was more wet than I expected but its intended effect was felt. I didn't take my eyes off of him for a few seconds.

He laughed. "I guess we both are lacking words then."

Remington speaking brought me out of my trance. "I guess so."

He could be so affectionate at times and that's the Remington I knew I had fallen in love with. The kind, caring, affectionate, intimate Remington.

Just as I finished talking, his phone dinged. Remington quickly glanced at me and I didn't give anything away, but I definitely wondered who was texting this time of the night. He seemed irritated when he read the text but he didn't respond. I also noticed that he put his ringer on silent. That was his usual mode of operation. I was surprised it even dinged in the first place. I could count on one hand how many times I've heard an actual notification on his phone.

When we arrived at my house I was exhausted. After a long work week and staying up late to work on my personal projects, I wanted nothing more than to get in my comfortable bed for a full eight to ten hours of sleep.

"I'm going to head upstairs to shower and get ready for bed," I said.

"I'll be up in a minute. I need to respond to a few emails and check the calendar for Slayton Graphics tomorrow."

"Okay, I'll see you in a few."

I showered and was fast asleep in no time. I'm not sure what time Remington decided to join me in bed. He did his usual; tapping me on my shoulder. I didn't pretend like I didn't want to get laid, but it was going to be the laziest lay. I was never too tired to turn down good sex. While the sex was good, he seemed off. After sex, I asked him what was on his mind. He didn't really answer. He just responded with, "You noticed, huh?"

Remington was the king of deflection and I wasn't dealing with it at almost 4:30 AM.

The next several months went by fast. Before I knew it, Remington and I had been dating for over a year. Everything we did was so natural. I almost lost track of time. We always made sure we made time for date nights which was helpful because we both had really crazy schedules.

Nicole and I worked diligently on marketing and promoting my book. I didn't realize all the work that went into getting a project ready for release. Because there was so much to do, we met almost every Saturday and at least one day during the week. Our Saturdays usually consisted of brunch and talking business. After we discussed what needed to get done for the upcoming week, we did the usual girl talk. We weren't best friends but she was cool to hang out with especially since we both were into fashion and loved to travel.

We met one Saturday after Nicole had returned from vacation in Mexico. We decided on brunch at a location in Midtown. After we finished discussing business, we enjoyed mimosas and talked.

"Girl, how was your vacation?"

"It was much needed. Very relaxing."

"Well-deserved. You look well rested."

And she did. Something looked different about her. I just couldn't figure out what it was yet.

"I needed that break. I work hard and play harder."

"I definitely understand that. I'm overdue for a vacation."

"I'm sure you are. I bet Remington is working you over time, too." She gave a small giggle after her comment.

"Girl, Remington barely looks up from his work these days. He's always working and hardly has time for anything else."

"Oh, he makes time for what he wants."

Her tone seemed a little off but then I could just be in my feelings because Remington was really working a lot.

"Don't we all make time for what we want?"

Nicole was looking off into space and she gave a distracted, "Yeah, that's true" response.

"Back to earth, Nicole." I waved my hands in an exaggerated motion.

"Oh sorry. Look, let's schedule a business meeting for Wednesday and we can see where we are with the never-ending to-do list."

"Sounds like a plan to me. Good catching up. We need to hit the outlet and shop one of these Saturdays instead of all this working."

"Agreed. Let that be a celebration after the successful release of your book."

"See you on Wednesday." I sat at the table a little confused on how Nicole's mood changed so quickly and how she abruptly ended our hang out. She seemed off but oh well. I continued to enjoy my bottomless mimosas.

At any rate, I was super excited and nervous about my upcoming book release. Just like I had mentioned to Nicole, Remington was buried deep into his own work. He seemed to always be working on something new. He was working diligently to form partnerships with other community leaders to open a center for at risk youth and young adults. The center allowed them to attend trade school and get on the right path through mentorships. I was so proud of him and the other leaders in the community that stepped up.

The Seduction

Remington and I had no issue intertwining our lives. We were pretty much cohabiting but we relished in the comfort of our own homes when one of us got on each other's nerves. And we did get on each other's nerves from time to time. I spent most of my time at his house, especially on the nights that he had the twins. His new business venture had him out more than usual. If it was his weekend to have the twins, I would babysit. It was easier than taking them to his sister and picking them up the next morning. The twins and I did fun activities together like plan tea parties, spa days/nights, lunch dates, etc.

One particular weekend, Remington and other community leaders were hosting a fundraising event for their new center. I knew it was important for me to attend the event. I also invited Brooklyn and Reign. I promised them that we would go out for drinks afterwards since we hadn't had the chance to hang out in a while. We all were busy with new boos and new adventures. I was stoked about the possibility of bar hopping and catching up with my girls. It was a Friday night so Peter Street would definitely be popping.

The event was held at the community center. I was amazed at how the center was transformed into this elegant event space that hosted more than three hundred community leaders, activists, and citizens. There were several sponsors for the event so I wasn't surprised to see Nicole as one of them. I noticed several other local businesses and politicians were listed as sponsors. There was also a silent auction being held. All funds raised went to sponsoring scholarships for community citizens interested in getting a trade.

The center was also set up as a job search hub. Not only did they provide resources on job searches and leads, but they provided the professional dress needed for interviews. In my opinion, the center gave Goodwill a run for its money. A lot went into making the center a one stop shop for the community. It was located in the heart of South Fulton.

It made me proud to know that all the services provided for that night were by black owned businesses in metro Atlanta. The food was catered by Hinley's and it was immaculate. I made a mental note to check them out for the surprise brunch we were hosting for Justice.

The night went on and everything was lovely. Brooklyn and Reign finally met Remington. They were blown away with his charisma and wit. I guess I had grown accustomed to it by now. He was just being Remington. After we mingled for a couple more hours, Brooklyn, Reign, and I decided to head out.

I was headed out the door when I literally bumped into Nicole. She wasn't paying attention and I was too busy running my mouth.

"Oh, hi, Nicole. Sorry."

"Hi, Alexis." She sounded a bit irritated.

"Is everything okay?"

"Yes, why do you ask?"

"You just seemed irritated," I said.

"I am. You know, men problems. They just won't do right."

"Yeah, that can be irritating. Hey, meet my two best friends, Brooklyn and Reign."

"Hi, Brooklyn and Reign. Nice to meet you. Alexis knows nothing about men problems. She has the perfect Remington."

Nicole said this with a smile that didn't quite meet her eyes. She seemed to be extremely irritated and I hope whatever is going on with her and her man gets handled quickly.

"Umm, he's far from perfect and he isn't my first rodeo. So, yeah I do."

"If you say so. Well, I'll see you around."

I ignored the irritated look on her face and the tone of her voice. "Umm, okay. I'm leaving so I'll see you at our next meeting. Have a great night."

"You're leaving the event before it's over and you're leaving your man here with all these women after him?"

"That's not my concern. He'll make the right decision. Have a good night, Nicole."

Brooklyn, Reign, and I exited the building.

Reign spoke up first, "What was her problem?"

"If I didn't know any better, I'd say she was jealous of you and Remington," Brooklyn said.

"I don't know what her problem is. Crazy part is she's never acted like that with me. So, that was just weird."

"She's hating but you let her know you weren't concerned about another female when it comes to Remington," Brooklyn said.

"Right! I'm not."

We continued our night and did the usual bar hopping on Peter Street. As if that wasn't enough, we decided to hit up a new hookah bar. It was dope as hell. The crowd wasn't too young and not too old either. The music was on point and the vibe was just nice. I decided to text Remington to see how the event ended.

Alexis: How did the event end? Hopefully, well.

I didn't get a response after like ten minutes so I decided to send another text. I know Remington had quite a few drinks.

Alexis: Hey, you good? Just checking since you didn't respond to my first text message.

Twenty minutes later and still no response. I decided not to trip. I just enjoyed the rest of my night with my girls. We got home way later than we expected. I showered and was knocked out.

It was around ten o'clock the next morning when I realized I still hadn't heard from Remington. I called but his phone went straight to his voicemail. I thought it was odd because he hardly ever let his phone die. I became slightly concerned but I didn't overreact. It was well after four o'clock and I still hadn't heard from Remington. Nicole's words played over and over in my head. Well, maybe he had taken one of the women up on their offer. I decided I had other things to be concerned with besides what a grown ass man was doing.

I called Brooklyn and Reign on three-way and we discussed the surprise brunch we were hosting for Justice. She had given birth to twin boys: Chance and Chase. She was overwhelmed so we decided to bring brunch to her. Honestly, Justice was an amazing mom and I was shocked at how well she adapted to such a huge responsibility. The twins looked just like Corey. Justice made the decision to take a year off while she got acclimated with having two newborn twins and their older daughter.

We decided on Hinley's for catering. Of course, we did the most southern of all menus: Fish & grits and chicken and waffles. Reign would pick up the fresh fruit. I'd grab some dessert and Brooklyn's ass volunteered to bring the alcohol. Why alcohol was an option is beyond me. Justice wasn't drinking while breastfeeding two very greedy little boys.

The brunch was scheduled for next Sunday and Corey had already been informed.

I was headed out to grab something to eat and just as I backed out of my garage, Remington pulled in behind me.

"Oh the dead has risen."

"Hi, Lexie! Where are you headed?"

"Hi. I'm headed to grab some dinner." I know Remington noticed the tone in which I spoke. The look on his face said as much. I didn't bother getting out of my car to hug him which was our normal.

"Umm, you want company?"

"Not really. I'm just doing a pick up order."

"Sorry about last night."

"What about it?"

"Sorry, I missed your messages. We had a situation to deal with after the event."

"Oh, cool. You could've just responded via text to let me know that instead of letting me worry about you but I'm happy you are okay."

Remington didn't realize how close he was to getting cussed out. The twitch in my right jaw alerted me to how mad I was.

"Come on, Lexie, it's not that serious."

"Sure, Remington. Move your car so I can go get my food before it's too cold to enjoy."

"Here, ride with me. I'll take you and I can tell you what happened with the money situation last night."

"You don't have to explain. I'm good."

"You're overreacting. I came by to explain."

"I just want to get my food and not worry about your disappearing act from last night."

"If you would have stayed you would have known what took place."

"Oh, it's my fault? Okay, Remington."

"That's not what I'm saying. Let's just get you some food and then maybe we can talk."

I didn't say anything as we headed to Mr. Everything to pick up my salmon and yellow rice plate. I actually made a point to not look at Remington. I looked out the passenger window at nothing in particular andsat with my arms folded across my chest. Remington didn't say much either. He had a grimace on his face. It baffled me that he had an attitude. The nerve of him. He just listened to the soft jazz music and we rode in silence. I was not feeling the vibe at all.

When we made it back to my house, Remington came in and began telling this story about how there was a discrepancy in the money from the silent auction. It sounded like someone had stolen money from the fundraiser. I listened intently but nowhere in the story did it reveal he had to stay all night and most of the next day reconciling the issue. I felt a shift in everything and I knew it wasn't an overreaction on my part.

Remington decided to stay over the rest of the day and the conversation was lackluster. I worked on the million and one projects that needed my attention and he was on his phone most of the time or asleep. Around midnight, I decided I was exhausted enough.

"Hey, I'm headed to bed," I said.

"I'll be up there in a few minutes. I'm sending out a few more invoices and responding to a few inquiries," Remington said.

I turned and headed up the stairs to my bedroom to get a quick hot shower and get in the bed. I was mentally and physically exhausted. I stepped into the hot shower and stood still under the pulsating shower head as I let all the tension from the day roll off. Just as I reached for my body wash and body scrub, Remington startled me when he opened the shower door.

He stepped in and quickly stepped back. "Damn, this water is too hot."

"I don't like lukewarm showers."

"We can warm up the shower another way." Remington brought his hand to rest on the center of my back. I quivered at his touch. It was a lot gentler than normal. "Lexie, you've been quiet most of the day."

"Yea, I just don't like the disappearing act you pulled last night and most of today."

"It wasn't a disappearing act. I told you what happened."

"Yeah, you did."

"So, what's the big deal?"

"The big deal is my gut says there is more."

If I was being honest, Nicole's words continued to play over and over in my head, too. It all had played a part in me believing Remington hadn't given me the full story.

"Let me make it up to you."

Remington placed small kisses at the nape of my neck. Again, I quivered at his luscious lips on my neck. My body defied me like always. There was a rush of heat that pooled in the apex of my thighs. Great! Just fucking great.

He slowly pulled me closer to him. His penis rested against my butt. It was rock hard and ready for action. I tried to ignore it but that coupled with the nape kissing made it impossible.

I relaxed more into his body and he nibbled on my earlobe. A moan accidentally slipped through my lips. I wanted nothing more than to have amazing shower sex with Remington and he knew it. In such a short amount of time, he had learned my body and how to get it to respond the way he wanted. As he continued to nibble on my earlobe, he used both his hands to pinch and tug at my nipples. It was a double sensation for me. He trailed kisses from my earlobe to my collarbone. I slowly turned to face him.

He devoured my mouth like never before and I matched his energy in the kiss. The pool of heat that settled between my thighs felt more like a fire by now. We broke off the kiss only to catch our breath. I rested my forehead on his chest. He lifted my chin.

"Alexis, what we have is rare and special. Don't let one off night mess that up."

I didn't respond. I just looked at him and smiled. He leaned in and kissed my forehead. At that moment, I knew Remington had me under a different spell. He reached around me and grabbed my aromatherapy body wash and bath sponge. After lathering the sponge, he continued to wash my body. Afterwards, I returned the favor for him.

We stepped out of the shower and grabbed our dry towels. I wrapped the towel around me and Remington pulled me toward him. He dried me off and proceeded to lotion my body. It was a mini massage and a turn on. I laid face down on the bed as he massaged and moisturized my back.

"Turn over, Lexie."

I obliged with no hesitation. He started with my feet and legs and made his way up to my thighs, inner thighs, lower stomach, and finally my breasts. He paid special attention to my breasts. He massaged them gently but made a gentle tug on my nipples. It was just enough to slightly sting but it was such a pleasurable feeling. A moan slipped through my lips each time he did his massage and tug thing. Initially, I tried to suppress the moan but after a while I wasn't interested in suppressing the pleasure it brought.

He replaced the massage and tug with his mouth. Rolling my nipples in his mouth and gently biting down. I was so overwhelmed by the sensation. I whimpered at the disconnect of Remington's mouth from my breast. He hovered over me, looking down at me with his infectious grin. I closed my eyes because I felt like he was searching my soul and I wasn't ready to bare it to him.

He captured my mouth with his and that was the beginning of an extraordinary night.

Remington didn't leave any part of my body unexplored by his tongue. I was in awe with the attention he paid to my body's cry for unmet needs. After several rounds of overwhelming sex, we settled into a nice slumber. It was short lived as Remington's phone started ringing at 4:45 AM. Startled, he answered it after several rings.

"Yes?" I couldn't make out the voice on the other end. However, Remington was already getting out of the bed and moving quickly. "I'll be there in fifteen minutes. Bye."

He seemed irritated.

"Is everything okay?" I asked.

"Yes, there's an issue at the office that needs to be handled. Let's do brunch tomorrow. I'll pick you up."

"Yeah, okay."

"Come on, Lexie. No attitude."

"I don't have an attitude. Do what you need to do."

He didn't say anything else. He kissed me on my forehead and left. I really didn't like the way he was moving this weekend.

Something was off and it was more than what he was telling me. I rolled over and hoped that sleep would find me. After more than an hour of tossing and turning, I decided to get up and attempt to write something.

I Wish

I wish you were here…physically you're present, but emotionally I wish you were here. I wish you were emotionally drawn to me the way I'm emotionally drawn to you. I wish your heart strings played the same sweet melody that mine does at the mention of your name. I wish you got the same butterflies as I do when I hear your voice. I wish you longed for my touch the way I long for yours. I wish your need for sweet nothing kisses was as strong as mine. I wish you would fall in love with an emotionally unavailable me and then maybe you'll understand my wishes. I wish you were here right now where I am emotionally. -A. Carter

I'm not even sure why I wrote what I wrote. I read it over and over several times. It's obviously how I felt about Remington. I hoped all was well with him and his office. I wouldn't reach out to him about brunch. I would let him take the lead on that. I decided to get up and head out for a run since the sun was finally rising. I ran a lot longer than I intended. My plan was to run three miles and I ended up doing seven. It wasn't an easy route either but I was pleasantly surprised with my speed and performance. I made it home, showered, and grabbed some fruit to eat.

Remington sent a text around 11 AM.

Remington: Hey Lexie, I'll be over in about 30 minutes.

Alexis: Cool, I'm dressed. See you then.

Remington: Wear comfortable clothes. I have plans for us after brunch.

Alexis: Yeah.

I fiddled around the house until Remington showed up. I didn't give him a chance to come in. I met him in the driveway. I didn't bring up the office situation because I wanted to see if he would bring it up. He didn't, so neither did I. The ride to Flying Biscuit in midtown was relatively quiet. We parked and made the short walk to the restaurant. It was crowded like always. I wasn't a fan of big crowds and in all honesty the food was overrated. Thank goodness for reservations. We headed inside and were seated less than ten minutes later.

Remington ordered a feast. Seriously, I thought he was expecting someone to join us with the amount of food he ordered for himself. I ordered my usual; waffle, turkey bacon, and home fries with a water with lemon. I was hungrier than usual after running seven miles.

We ate in an awkward silence for the most part before I decided to break it.

"So, what's the plan for after brunch?"

"I thought we could rent Segway cruzers and tour Eastside Atlanta."

"Oh okay, sounds fun."

Honestly, my anxiety skyrocketed through the roof. I was sure I was going to be a nervous wreck but I looked forward to the adventure. We finished our brunch and headed back to the car.

"Don't be nervous baby."

"What makes you think I'm nervous?"

"Alexis, I know you better than you think I know you. Whenever you get nervous you do this little twitch with your finger and you always have beads of sweat pop up on your nose. You need more evidence?"

"I just don't know about riding the Segway in the street."

"Don't you ride your bike in the street?"

"Yes, it's different though."

"How is it different?"

"I don't know. I'm more comfortable on my bike."

"You don't know how comfortable you'll be on the Segway."

"I just get nervous thinking about downtown Atlanta traffic."

"Trust me baby. I'm not going to push you too far pass your limit."

"You don't know what limits are. You are the king of going too far."

"I only like to test your limits but I know what's too far for you. Give me your hand."

Reluctantly, I gave Remington my hand and he just held it. Arrogantly he said, "I know my touch is your calming mechanism."

I just grinned at him because he was correct but I would never tell him that.

Remington drove the short distance holding my hand.

It only took minutes to arrive at the meetup for the Segway tour. After a few minutes practicing, we were on our way. The tour took us through Inman Park, Atlanta's first planned suburb established in the 1890s. The houses were awesome over there and they came with a nice price tag. After passing through Inman Park, we entered Cabbagetown, a cute neighborhood in Atlanta. I enjoyed the art mural. We entered Oakland cemetery, the city's oldest public cemetery. It had been on my list of places to visit. During Halloween, the cemetery is often turned into a haunted cemetery. I was most excited about the cemetery. I was in awe and had this stupid grin on my face.

"You are so weird."

"Weird? Why would you say that?"

"Who gets this excited about a cemetery?"

"It's not the cemetery. It's the history of it."

"Again, just weird."

"I'm not weird. I'm inquisitive and have a love for history."

"It's okay. You're my kind of weird."

Remington leaned in for a kiss. I expected it to be a quick brush across the lips but to my surprise it was a real kiss. My body betrayed me and a soft moan escaped my lips. Remington pulled back and looked at me.

"Watch how you respond to me. I'd hate for the dead to hear you moaning the rest of the evening."

I just gave him a school girl giggle and said, "Boy hush. Let's finish this tour."

Part of the Segway tour took us on the Atlanta Beltline where we passed by several local restaurants. Remington and I stopped and got a popsicle from King of Pops. Our final stop was Martin Luther King Jr. National Park and his childhood home. The total tour time was only eight miles but it was the most interesting eight miles I'd experienced in Atlanta thus far.

I had finally gotten the hang of operating the Segway when we returned. We decided to walk a little before heading back to my side of town. The walk began in silence. Remington broke the silence this time.

"There was a slight incident at the office last night with Nikki and someone else."

"Who is Nikki?"

"Nicole."

I didn't say anything to Remington but calling her Nikki seemed really intimate in my eyes. Only my close friends and family call me Lexie. All my business partners call me Alexis. This was my first time hearing Remington call Nicole Nikki and it just seemed weird. Out of line even.

"Oh really? Why was she at the office that time of the night?"

"I have no idea. You know how you creatives work all times of the night."

"Yeah, but I don't leave my house and go to an office to work. What type of incident?"

"Personal and I'd rather not divulge."

I stopped abruptly. "Well, why bring it up?"

"So you can stop being so pissy."

I stepped in front of Remington and brought my hands to my hips. "I'm not being pissy. I just don't like how you've been moving this weekend."

"What are you talking about?"

"Disappearing acts and middle of the night phone calls but hey, do you." I rolled my eyes and started back walking at a much faster pace.

"Okay, Lexie. What you have planned for later?"

I was so damn frustrated with Remington and I know he knew it. He was being real nonchalant but I know if I moved the way he's been moving all weekend he would be on another level of pissed.

"I think I'm going to do some work and find me a good book to read."

"Oh, do it at my house then. I have some work I need to do but I would love to have your company."

"I'll let you know."

This time Remington stepped in front of me. I stumbled into him.

"Come on, Lex! You are being difficult for no reason."

I rolled my eyes and stepped around him. I decided not to respond to his comment. I would decide later if I was going to Remington's to spend the night. My upcoming week would be a long week and I needed to be on point. Remington seemed to be taking up too much headspace at the moment. I needed a clear head and he clouded my judgement.

Remington dropped me off at home.

"Let me know if you plan to come by and I can order takeout."

"I'll let you know."

He drove off and I went inside. I decided to take a hot shower and relax. Just as I was getting out the shower I received a text message from Nikki.

Nikki: Hey Alexis. I'm not sure if Remington told you but I will no longer be working with Slayton Graphics. I've sent all the information to you via email so you can have it for the next person. It has been a pleasure working with you and good luck becoming a household name.

I didn't respond immediately because I didn't know what to say. What the good got damn fuck? Remington needed to give a better explanation as to what was going on because it was now affecting me.

Alexis: Hi Nikki. I'm sorry to hear this. I'm fine with still working with you even if you are not working with Slayton's Graphics. I would hate to start over with someone new. You've been doing a phenomenal job.

I received an instant response from Nikki which I wasn't expecting.

Nikki: Alexis, I appreciate it but I think it's best we cut all ties. I'm informing all my clients that I'm leaving Slayton's Graphics. Unfortunately, it means cutting ties with all clients as well. I think it will cut down on the confusion.

Alexis: Thanks. Good luck. I know you will be great wherever you go.

Nikki: Thanks and take care.

Just like that I was almost back at square one. I needed to find another branding specialist and quick. I also decided that I would go to Remington's house after all. I needed him to provide a better explanation than what he'd given earlier. Hell, earlier he didn't even mention Nikki not working with them anymore. There has to be more to the story than what's being told.

I packed an overnight bag after finally getting dressed. I did a few things around the house before sitting down for a minute to gather my thoughts. I sent Remington a text to let him know I would be over around 8:30. I still had a few minutes to spare so I sent a group text to Brooklyn and Reign. We chatted for way longer than I expected. Around 8:10, I headed to Remington's. Luckily, I wasn't too far away. When I was enroute he text to let me know that he left the door unlocked and to let myself in as he was picking up food from Olive Garden. He hadn't bothered to ask what I wanted so I'm assuming he got my usual order; grilled salmon, fettuccine alfredo, and broccoli.

I pulled into Remington's driveway and just sat in the car for a few minutes. I finished listening to my ratchet trap music before heading inside. I loved the nice cozy ambience of his house. While he had an open concept, his living space wasn't too open. The warm décor colors in both rooms made it even more inviting. My favorite feature in his home was the fireplace. I also enjoyed the masculine aroma in his home. I could tell he had been cleaning. It smelled fresh and there was a basket of unfolded laundry in the living room. I put my things in his room and went back to the living room. Out of habit, I grabbed the basket of laundry and started to fold them.

Remington walked in just as I was finishing the load of laundry.

"Hey, Lexie." Remington kissed my forehead.

"Hi, Remington." I adjusted myself slightly to give him a kiss on the lips. He smiled a boyish grin.

"I should've known you would fold the clothes. You just can't let stuff be out of place."

I gave a half smile and settled back into my seat on the sofa. I ignored his comment and didn't waste any time getting what little details I could about Nikki.

"Nikki texted me today."

"What did she want?" I could hear the irritation in his voice and see the twitch in his jawline. Oh shit, this must be bad.

"She dropped me as a client."

"She did what?" Remington was now visibly clenching his jaw.

"So, you didn't know? She said she was no longer working with Slayton's Graphics and unfortunately it meant leaving her clients."

"She's a nutcase. I know a few other brand specialists...Crazy ass girl." He seemed to visibly relax after I gave him that tad bit of information.

"So, are you going to tell me what happened?"

"It's not for me to tell. It's her personal business."

"Really, Remington? I deserve to know something since it is affecting me now."

"It won't affect you. I know other brand specialists who are just as good as she is, if not better."

"Remington, it still affects me. I have to build a relationship with someone else in the middle of launching my book and all the other shit."

"Lexie, you are making a big deal out of it for nothing." I know he was frustrated but I was trying to figure out if he was frustrated with my persistence or just the Nicole situation altogether.

"Whatever, Remington. I'm ready to eat so I can get settled and relax before bed."

"Fine, Lex! I ordered your usual. I also have some wine in the fridge if you want it." Remington's voice was slightly elevated and I really didn't appreciate it.

"I'll take a glass or two. Thanks."

We made small talk while eating but the vibe was off. It wasn't our usual relaxed conversation about any and everything. This whole weekend was just a mystery. Something was off. Way off. After dinner, Remington cleared the table and gave me a forehead kiss before announcing he was headed to his office to do some work. I relaxed on his sectional in the living room, watching HGTV. I fell asleep and was awakened by Remington slightly shaking me.

"Come on, Lex. Let's go to bed."

"Okay, I need to take another shower before bed."

"I ran us a hot bath if you want to join me."

"Oh, okay."

Remington let me get in the bath first and he slid in behind me. The water was warmer than what he usually runs and I appreciated it very much. I relaxed into him and closed my eyes as he sponged warm water to the front of my body. It felt great to be so relaxed after such an odd weekend.

"This has been a weird weekend."

"Don't give it too much thought. Let's relax for the upcoming week."

I didn't utter another word and did just what he requested. I relaxed into him and enjoyed his touch. We exited the bath after the water had gotten too cold for me. Remington dried me off and moisturized me from head to toe. I returned the favor of moisturizing him and tracing some of my favorite places on his body with my tongue. We ended a weird weekend with amazing sex. He seemed to be physically and emotionally present. It was a different feeling. One I enjoyed very much.

Monday arrived way too quickly for me. Remington was up in a flash with no hesitation as I struggled to get out of the bed. I braced myself for a long day. I made a peanut butter and jelly and grabbed a cup of hot tea. Remington enjoyed his oatmeal with sausage and a cup of coffee.

"Remington, I'm leaving. Have a good day!" I yelled on my way out of the door. I didn't wait for a response because I was really close to being late and I had a meeting first thing this morning. I was barely out of the driveway when my phone rang with Remington's ringtone.

"Hey Remington. I said bye."

"I know. I meant to let you know I'm setting up appointments with you and a few other brand specialists this week. I'll email you a few different times. Let me know what works for you."

"Oh okay. Thanks."

"Lex, you have to trust me. There's a method to my madness. Just trust me. I'll talk to you later."

"I'll talk to you later. Have a good day."

The drive to work was hectic. I hated Atlanta traffic. It was so unpredictable. A thirty-minute commute can turn into an hour and half commute on any day. I was sure I was going to be late for my meeting. Just as I was getting ready to call my colleague, I received an email stating the meeting had been pushed back. Look at God! I relaxed knowing I had some extra time to spare now. Luckily, I was well prepared for the meeting and didn't need to do anything additional.

After being stuck in my car forty minutes longer than usual, I made it to the downtown office. I rushed in and put my things down, needing to get to the restroom as soon as possible. I already had a cup of hot tea and two bottles of water. My bladder was screaming. I made it to the restroom just in time to prevent an accident. Feeling much better, I walked back to my desk and got ready to head into the conference room with my laptop. My phone dinged and I noticed I had emails from Remington and a text from him as well.

Remington: Sent you the emails. Respond when you can. Dinner at your place?

Alexis: Thanks, I'll check it out. Yeah, we can do dinner at my house.

Remington: See you later. Oh yeah, listen to this.

He attached a YouTube video of Miguel's *Adorn*. I smiled and put on my game face for my meeting. I had meeting after meeting that day. Work was exhausting and at three o'clock I decided I was calling it a day. I packed up my laptop and headed out of the office. I hadn't eaten lunch or anything. Starved and grouchy, I stopped by Publix grocery store on the way home and grabbed some fish and seafood. I would make something quick and simple. When I made it home, I cut potatoes to make French fries as a snack until I cooked dinner. I laid on the couch and fell asleep. I was awakened by my ringing phone. It was Remington.

"Hey Remington," I answered, groggily.

"Hey. I'm on my way over. Are you cooking or should I pick up something?"

"No, I'm cooking. I'm getting up now. I slept longer than expected."

"I'll be there in about 30."

"Okay, I'll just be finishing up the food by then."

I hung up with Remington and went into the kitchen to start cooking. I started shrimp and grits for Remington and grilled fish for me. I also made a vegetable medley of squash, zucchini, carrots, and green beans. I had let the garage up a few minutes earlier for Remington. I had another few minutes on my grilled fish and dinner would be ready.

"Hey Remington. Dinner will be ready in a few minutes."

"Okay, I'm going to wash my hands and put my things upstairs."

Remington came back downstairs and helped set the table. He decided he wanted something stronger than wine to go with his dinner while I enjoyed a cold glass of cabernet. Remington finally broke the silence that had settled into the room.

"Did you get a chance to look at the emails I sent earlier?"

"Not yet, it's on my to-do list tonight after dinner. Work was crazy with meeting after meeting and I was exhausted when I made it home, hence me oversleeping."

"Yeah, let's move quickly on the appointments so it won't be a lag in anything that you were planning."

"Are you going to at least tell me what happened with Nikki?"

"Lex, it's not important and I don't want to spend a lot of energy discussing it."

"Hmph, okay."

An awkward silence fell over the room again. I enjoyed the rest of my dinner and glass of wine. Remington finished his food in record time and went back for seconds. I always cooked way too much food. It was a bad habit from cooking in college that I hadn't quite broken yet. Honestly, I didn't know how to cook in small portions so there were always leftovers.

"This shrimp and grits is good. I'm happy there's enough for me to have for lunch tomorrow."

"You need to start bringing your own containers because you haven't returned any of mine and I'm not going to buy new ones."

"I'll order you new ones because I don't want to hear your mouth about the fact that I can't find the tops to the containers now."

"How? How do you misplace the tops? But yes, order me some new ones. I'll send you the ones I want."

"Okay, I need to do some work for a little bit but while I'm thinking about it check your schedule for three weeks out. I want to go to Virginia and hang with my folks."

"Umm, okay. Are you taking the girls?"

"Yes, I'll pick them up the night before and we will fly out the next morning. I want to make sure you'll be free to go."

"Is it too soon for me to meet your folks?"

"Nope, if it were you wouldn't be meeting them. Don't overthink this either."

He kissed me on the neck and headed upstairs. That one gesture warmed my body temperature by a couple degrees. I cleaned the kitchen and decided to head upstairs to my office so I could work on a few things before I got too caught up in Remington. He definitely kept me under his spell.

I entered my office to find Remington occupying it. I didn't need any distractions and his masculine scent alone was a distraction. I grabbed my laptop to head back to the living room.

"Where are you going?"

"I'm headed downstairs so we can both work with little to no distractions."

"But I like your kind of distraction."

"We can be distractions later. You seem to be engrossed in your work and I need to get engrossed in my many projects and respond to emails."

"I'll hold you to that."

I lost track of time while working downstairs. I was working diligently and was startled when I heard Remington talking louder than usual on the phone. From the sound of it he was pissed off. I made my way upstairs to see what was going on and he was sitting in front of the computer on a video conference. I'm not sure who he was on a teleconference with because the person had their camera off. My first thought was why video conference if you aren't going to have the video on, but whatever.

"Hey, is everything okay?"

"Yes!" he snapped.

"Well, you were loud and I'm just making sure nothing is wrong."

"Lex, I'm fine. I'm about to finish and I can come downstairs to chill with you in a bit."

He was very dismissive in his statement. I was not in the mood to start an argument about something so non-trivial. I turned and left the room. When I got back downstairs I noticed I had several missed phone calls from an unknown number. Weird because I usually don't get unknown numbers calling. Bot calls and telemarketing, but not unknown. I got back into my groove of working while enjoying music from my iPad. When I looked up again it was almost midnight. I had no intentions of staying up this late. I made my way upstairs to see if Remington was still working. He wasn't in the office space. When I went into my bedroom he was laid across the bed asleep.

He must have been tired. He never made it downstairs to chill. I showered quickly and got dressed for bed. So much for being a distraction tonight. I gently shook him awake so he could get under the covers. I could tell he wasn't in a good mood. I don't know if it was because I woke him up or if he was still upset from his phone conversation earlier. Either way he was in a pissy mood. There went the possibility of sex.

We slept like an old married couple who didn't really like each other. It was weird. He was there physically but intimately he was unavailable. I was so accustomed to sleeping with some part of my body touching his that I didn't sleep well. I woke up grouchy as ever the next morning. Remington wasn't his usual bubbly self and it was a quiet morning for us. I dressed quickly and headed out the door in hopes of beating some of the rush hour traffic.

The next couple weeks were off for Remington and I. He was physically present yet he always seemed to be mentally, emotionally, and intimately unavailable. I could tell when Remington was just present. He didn't actively engage in conversation and most of the time it was like I was talking to myself. I would intentionally say something off the wall and he wouldn't respond. That's how I knew when he was just present. While we were having sex, it was just that - sex. Nothing passionate or anything to write home about. I asked a few times what was going on and he said he was working through some personal issues so I let it be.

It was finally the week that we were traveling to Virginia so I could meet his folks. Remington made it back to Atlanta late Wednesday night from picking the girls up in Charlotte. I'm still not sure why he had to drive all the way and they didn't meet at the halfway point. I decided to stay at his house since the flight was so early in the morning. I had already packed bags for the girls and I.

The early morning flight was a hassle with two kids. They were grouchy and so was I. Remington seemed to be back in his happy place. We landed in Virginia Beach, VA, around 9:30 AM. The girls and I headed to baggage claim while Remington headed to the rental car counter.

"Lexie, I will meet you all outside the terminal." He handed me his personal phone while he took a call on his business line.

"Just call me when you are close so we can let you know where we will be standing."

"Okay," Remington said, distracted. I hope this was not an indication of how he was going to be during the trip. There is nothing more annoying than a distracted Remington. I know the girls would not appreciate it much.

"Lexie, what are we going to do?" Reagan asked.

"I'm not sure. Your dad hasn't told me much but whatever it is I'm sure it will be fun."

"I hope our cousins will be here, too. Maybe Grandpa and Grandma, too," Alivia chimed in.

I hadn't really thought about how little Remington had told me about this trip. I didn't know what I was walking into today. Was it a family reunion or just he and his siblings with their kids? He had been very tight-lipped about this whole trip. My thoughts were interrupted by his ringing phone. I forgot I was even holding it. I looked down and saw it was Nikki calling. I thought it was odd but I didn't bother answering it. She would call his business line if it was that important. Why hadn't she called that number anyway? I was pulled out of my thoughts by Alivia asking a question.

"Can we get something to eat? I'm hungry."

"Me, too," Reagan chimed in.

"We will stop and get food when we are on our way to the hotel."

"Dad said we were staying in a big house with a swimming pool and a backyard."

"Hotels are boring and I want to get in the pool," Reagan said.

"Okay, if your dad said we're staying in a big house then I'm sure we are staying in a big house." I should've asked more questions about this trip instead of blindly trusting Remington. I hope it's nothing too crazy or too many people. We grabbed our bags off the carousel and headed toward the door to wait for Remington to pick us up. After ten minutes or so of waiting, the girls were getting antsy and complaining even more about food. My phone finally dinged with a text message from Remington.

Remington: I'm headed your way. I'm in a black Navigator.

Alexis: Okay, we are standing outside Delta terminal at the first gate. The girls are hungry so we need to stop to get some food.

Remington didn't respond, not that I expected him to. Just as he was pulling up, his phone began to ring again. This time it was an unknown number. I handed him his phone and he just shook his head. He grabbed our bags while the girls and I got in the car.

"Dad, can we stop and get something to eat?" Alivia asked. "I'm hungry."

"Me too!" Reagan all but screamed.

"No, your aunts have cooked food so we can eat when we get to the house."

"Who all will be here this weekend?" I asked.

"It's just my siblings and their families. It's our annual getaway."

"Oh, okay."

I wasn't sure how I felt about meeting Remington's sisters but I'm here now. I guess it's better than unexpectedly meeting his parents. The drive was about twenty minutes before we pulled into an extremely nice subdivision. The girls were in awe of the houses. They said some of them looked like castles and honestly they did. We pulled into the grand driveway of our AirBnB and the house was nothing short of a mansion.

The girls hurriedly opened the truck and got out. They all but sprinted to the door.

"Alivia and Reagan, come get your bags!" I yelled.

Remington laughed. "Don't worry about it. I'll grab all the bags in a little bit. Let's get inside so I can introduce you to Trouble 1 and Trouble 2." I laughed nervously. Remington and I had been in our own little bubble for so long that I wasn't sure about letting anyone outside of the girls into our world. "Please don't tell me you're nervous about meeting my sisters?"

"It's just...I wasn't prepared to stay in the same house as them. I mean I knew I would meet your folks but I didn't realize we would all be slumber partying together."

Remington cupped my face between his hands. "Hey, you'll be fine. When you start to feel overwhelmed we can always retire to the bedroom for a little cross training."

"Or we can come out and walk around the neighborhood for some fresh air. I'm not sure I want to have sex with you with a house full of your folks."

"Lexie, get used to the idea. I'm not lying beside you all weekend without cross training." He winked and pulled my hand for me to head into the house with him. Reluctantly, I obliged.

"Hi Alexis! I'm Santoria and this is my sister, Synthia."

"Synthia with an S."

"Hi, Santoria and Synthia. Nice to meet you."

"Well damn, give me a chance to introduce you to Alexis...Lexie, these are the two thorns in my side that I complain about frequently."

"Yeah but you wouldn't trade us for anything in the world," Synthia boasted.

"Nothing in this world. Anyway, Lexie, make yourself comfortable. I'm going to speak to my niece and nephews before I head out to get the bags."

"I can help you grab the bags if you need me to."

"Nah, I'm good. Get acquainted with these two and I'll be back shortly." Remington brushed a light kiss across my lips and zipped off down the hallway. I stood in silence as his sisters assessed me from head to toe. It was awkward but I was not backing down so I began to look at them in the same manner. They both burst into laughter.

"I like you," Santoria blurted out.

"Me too," Synthia agreed.

"Why is that?" I asked, nonchalantly.

"Because you won't take Remington's shit. I can tell by how you stared back at us," Synthia said.

"Don't worry. You pass the test. Plus, I know the girls really like you," Satoria added.

I playfully rolled my eyes. "Glad I could pass your test." Honestly, I knew I would like them. "What's on the agenda for this weekend? Anything special?"

"Once our menfolk get here we will do what we usually do when we have these gatherings. We are just going to hang out here, cook, and enjoy each other's company," Santoria said.

"Yeah but the problem is we promised the kids a day at the beach so we need to block off a morning to do that because I will not be at the beach in the heat of the day," Synthia said.

"Who's the oldest between the two of you?"

"Synthia is but only by two minutes."

"Wait, y'all are twins?"

"Yes," they sang in unison.

"Remington never said y'all were twins. How cool is that?"

Santoria rolled her eyes. "Not cool at all. You have no idea the headache this chick is."

"Whatever, you wouldn't know what to do without me."

"As much as I would like to continue this conversation right here, I need to get in the kitchen so we can get to making food for the kiddos and Remington," Santoria said.

We headed towards the kitchen. Synthia started to pull eggs, bacon, sausage, and butter out of the refrigerator. Santoria had pancake mix in her hands. I guess we're eating breakfast food.

"What do y'all need me to help with?"

"Do you want to make French toast or biscuits?" Santoria asked.

"Either is fine with me. Remington doesn't like can biscuits though."

Synthia laughed. "We aren't the only ones who have Remington spoiled."

"Yeah, we know he likes his biscuits from scratch," Santoria said.

"Let's just do French toast," I said.

"That works," they both said.

We moved around the kitchen easily. It was safe to say that Synthia and Santoria knew how to cook as well. Remington appeared in the kitchen with a big kool-aid grin on his face.

"I love watching three of my favorite women in the kitchen. Now, I'm just missing Mom and Grandma."

I smiled and continued with my task of making French toast. Honestly, I decided on French toast because from the items Synthia pulled from the refrigerator I ate none of it. I'm not a big breakfast food eater. I didn't eat pork or eggs. So, French toast would be my saving grace in this situation. I'm hoping they have some kind of fruit.

"Well, it's your lucky weekend. Mom and Dad will be here later tonight. Grammy couldn't make it but at least you get Mom," Synthia said.

"Of course, they wouldn't miss the opportunity to see their favorite child and all their grands under one roof."

"Whatever," Synthia laughed.

I noticed Santoria wasn't saying much. I thought it was odd since they all seemed so close.

"Hey, are you okay?" Remington asked Santoria.

"Yeah, I'm just mentally preparing for the onslaught of questions and odd looks. You know mom can be so judgmental."

"Well, at least you have dad on your side. We both know you're his favorite child."

"I can handle Dad. Mom is my problem. She's going to be so rude to David and it's going to put a damper on things."

"Let's think positive. Remington and I will play tag team when she starts to act an ass," Synthia said.

"Thanks guys. I appreciate it. I just don't want this to be awkward and I really need a relaxing weekend. The last six months have been hell," Santoria said.

There was such a sad tone in her voice. Since I didn't know what was going on I almost felt like I was eavesdropping. I excused myself from the room so they could continue their private conversation. At least, a conversation I felt like should have been private. I was headed down the hall trying to find a bathroom when I ran into Reagan and the cutest little boy.

"Lexie, look at my cousin. His name is DJ and he is two." DJ held up two fingers and giggled.

"Hey handsome! Reagan, what are y'all up to?"

"Nothing, I'm hungry. Are my aunties done cooking?"

"Not yet but they will be in a minute. I'll come get you when the food is done."

"Okay. Lexie, can I have a snack. You packed snacks in our bag didn't you?"

"Yes, baby but it's too early for snacks. I'll see if there is any fruit and bring it to you and the others in the backyard."

"Okay."

Reagan was ready to eat. Let me find this child some type of snack before she perished. I finally found the bathroom. Thankfully because my bladder was screaming. I also made a mental note to take a tour of the house so I won't be wandering around like a stranger. Technically, I was a stranger to everyone but Remington and the girls. After my extended restroom break, I headed back to the kitchen.

When I walked into the room I could instantly tell the mood had changed back to the happy go lucky mood before my departure.

"Where did you run off to?" Remington asked.

Before I could respond Santoria chimed in. "She probably didn't want to hear about the family drama that's sure to ensue."

"I went to the restroom and ran into Reagan and DJ in the hallway. Reagan is starving." I glared at Remington. "You should've gotten them something to eat this morning."

"She will be okay. We will all be sitting down to eat soon."

"Actually, we can call them in now. We can just get them washed up and start with fruit while the bacon finishes up," Synthia said.

"Oh snap, I need to finish the French toast."

"The French toast is for the adults. These kids are getting these pancakes," Synthia said.

Remington went to gather the kids and get them cleaned up before bringing them into the kitchen. Synthia, Santoria, and I made small talk as we finished up breakfast and started making plates for the kids. Naturally, I fixed Alivia and Reagan's plate. I didn't realize how many kids were in the house. Santoria had three kids: Samaria, 6;

Slayton, 4; and DJ 2. Synthia had two boys: Deuce 4; and Amir, 3.

Remington didn't bother sitting the kids at the dining room table. He just had them sit in a circle on the floor and we handed out plates. Just like him to do the easiest thing. I looked at him and shook my head. He smiled and winked. The four adults made their way back into the kitchen and we each fixed our plates. I had French toast and fruit.

"I'm offended. Is that all you're eating, French toast and fruit? So, you don't trust our cooking?" Synthia asked.

"Nah, I don't eat eggs or pork."

"Oh hell. Remington you didn't want to tell us that? We could've picked up turkey products," Santoria said.

"Shit, Lexie is too picky. We are just going to make a grocery store run so she can get what she likes. I wasn't going to have y'all wasting your time trying to figure it out. Hell, I don't know what she likes after all this time."

"Whatever. I'm not picky. I just like what I like."

"Well, at least it's not that she doesn't trust our cooking. I was going to be so offended

and take back my statement of liking you,"
Santoria said.

While both Santoria and Synthia were
outspoken, I could tell that Santoria was the
more outspoken one between the two. I
wonder if she was like that with her mom. I
guess I would find out later that day. We all
sat at the table and enjoyed the food we
had prepared. The conversation was easy
and before long I felt like I had known his
sisters way longer than a couple of hours.
Synthia was the comedian in the family and
she was very protective of her siblings. She
all but catered to Remington. She got up
from the table twice: once to pour him more
orange juice and a second time to put on a
pot of coffee for him. Hmph, this is where he
gets all that spoiled mess from. I can't
imagine how his mom and grandma catered
to him if his sister is doing all this. Santoria
wasn't under Remington's spell so much.

I glanced up and noticed that Santoria
seemed to be in deep thought from time to
time. It was clear something was on her
mind. There was also a sadness in her
eyes. For some odd reason, I was drawn to
her. After breakfast, I cleaned up the mess
the kids made and Synthia cleared the table
from the adults. Surprisingly, Remington

agreed to load the dishwasher. Santoria had gone upstairs to put DJ down for his nap.

I stood at the French doors that led to the backyard watching the kids run wild and carefree. Remington startled me when he walked up behind me and flicked his tongue on my earlobe. My body temperature instantly rose three degrees.

"What are you doing?"

"Trying to get your attention. I called your name twice and you didn't even notice."

"Oh sorry. What do you need?"

"You."

"Remington, seriously what do you need?"

"I'm being serious, Lexie. I need to cross train before my parents get here. I need to relieve some stress and relax."

"Umm, can we go for a jog or workout or something?"

"Nah, we are cross training so you decide where. But it's happening within the next five minutes."

"It's like you're bullying me into sex."

"I'm actually doing us both a favor. You are most relaxed after sex and I need to relieve some stress. You still seem a little nervous."

"I'm a little nervous about meeting your parents but I don't think sex will fix that."

"Only one way to find out. So, bring your ass."

We literally had this whole conversation with his tongue periodically flicking my earlobe. He knew what he was doing. He knew nothing besides kissing got me ready to have sex like kissing me on my earlobe. I would be lying if I said I wasn't in the mood. I was apprehensive but the pool of heat at the apex of my thighs was slowly winning.

He pulled me by the waist and drew me even closer to him. Not that I needed to be any closer. I knew I was going to submit to his request. We headed upstairs to the bedroom where we would sleep and obviously sex each other for the next three or four days. The room was so spacious and nicely decorated. The black and white décor with pops of color wasn't too feminine or masculine. It was an excellent balance. We made our way to the California King bed and Remington was like a horny teenager. He was moving too fast and fumbling over getting my clothes off.

"Damn, slow down. This is not setting the mood for me."

"The mood was set downstairs when my tongue caressed your earlobe."

"It was not. I know we need to be quick but damn don't make it feel like it's nothing more than a bathroom fuck."

"Sorry. You know it'll be more than that."

Remington slowed his pace a little and we found our rhythm with our kiss. It was no secret that I was more than ready for sex with him. My feminine scent filled the room but Remington liked to check my readiness by running his fingers at the apex of my thighs. My body constantly defied me. Whenever I was turned on by Remington a pool of heat and sweat settled between my thighs. It was almost embarrassing.

"Hmmm, you're so ready for me, Lexie. You know I like when you are ready for me."

"Umm, hmm." That was all I managed to get out of my mouth. Remington straddled me and I wrapped my legs around his waist. He paused and looked down at me for longer than I found to be necessary. He blinked and shook his head slightly.

"What's the problem, Remington?"

"Nothing, I just had a thought."

"About what?"

"Nothing important, Alexis."

Funny, he never calls me Alexis. I let it go because honestly my body was screaming with unmet needs. I'd probe later but right now my main concern was getting my fill of Remington. The sex was amazing and lasted way longer than either of us anticipated. A few times I caught Remington just staring at me. It was weird but I was too caught up in the moment to ask questions. I was so thankful that our bedroom had an ensuite so I wouldn't have to travel the walk of shame to the restroom to shower.

Remington joined me in the shower. I should've expected that from him.

"Damn, this water is too hot, Lexie."

"It's not. This is how I like my water in the shower. I hate lukewarm showers."

"It doesn't have to be set to a temp equivalent to hell."

"Remington, have you been to hell?"

"No, but I've been through hell." I didn't respond. I rolled my eyes. "Your eyes are going to get stuck like that."

"Like what?" I asked, coyly.

"Come on, Lexie, I know you rolled your eyes. I know you better than you think."

I really wanted to enjoy my shower. He was in here complaining about the temperature of the water and now he was talking about my eye rolling habit. I just shook my head. Remington sponged water on my back. I passed him my body wash and he lathered the sponge. He began to wash my back and I sank into his front. That wasn't a good idea. His penis poked me in my back.

"Damn."

"You knew this was going to happen."

Remington eased into me and I was taken aback by his gentleness. He nibbled on my ear before leaning in to draw circles on my neck with his tongue. I didn't stand a chance with him when he made me feel this good. At that moment, I noticed that he was inside of me but was not moving. I moaned his name and he began to move ever so slowly. The whole experience was so sensual. I was so lost that I barely noticed he was whispering in my ear.

"What did you say?"

"Which part do I need to repeat?"

Embarrassingly, I said, "All of it."

"I said you make me a better person. These past few months with you have been amazing. Nothing has compared."

"Oh." That was all I could manage to say. I really was at a loss for words. Remington leaned closer and continued to whisper in my ear while increasing his speed.

"You're mine and I'm not letting you go. Lexie, do you understand what I'm saying?"

"Umm, yes."

"No, Alexis Carter, do you understand what I'm saying?"

By this time, Remington was pounding into me at a much faster and harder pace. It was hard to concentrate on what he was saying and doing to my body at the same time. I needed to choose what I was going to focus on and as much as I wanted to understand what he was saying my body said I needed what he was doing more than the words he was speaking.

"Yes, Remington I understand."

"What am I saying, Alexis?"

"I'm yours." I was a second away from my orgasm when Remington stilled and the pounding stop. "Why did you stop? I'm so close to coming."

"You're not paying attention to me. I need you to understand me and I'm not giving you what you want until you hear me."

"I hear you. I understand you. Now, let me cum."

"No, you don't. You are mine, Alexis. I love you."

My body stilled at his declaration. This is what he has been trying to get me to understand. Oddly, his confession was a buzzkill on my libido. I had so many questions running through my mind. It was hard to focus.

"Do you understand me now, Alexis Carter? You are mine."

I didn't say anything. I just stood frozen with way too many thoughts running through my mind. Why is he telling me this now? Why does he sound so possessive? Does he really love me? Do I say I love you back?

Remington didn't seem to mind my silence. He pulled out and turned me to face him. He slowly entered me again and demanded that I wrap my legs around his waist. He pivoted and slowly walked until my back was against the wall. He began his relentless pounding again and while I wanted to enjoy the moment I couldn't. My thoughts were running wild. A few short minutes after his confession, Remington was whispering my name while he came inside of me. I slowly released my legs from his waist. He stared at me intently as if he was trying to see into my soul. For the first time ever, I felt embarrassed to be standing naked with him. I walked in front of him with my back to his front so the water could run over my body. I showered quickly and got out of the shower. Remington stayed in and enjoyed his lukewarm shower.

Suddenly, I felt exhausted. That wasn't unusual because ninety-nine percent of the time after sex with Remington I would fall right to sleep. This wasn't the same kind of feeling. I just felt tired and weary, not sexually exhausted. I dressed quickly and curled up in the middle of the bed for a quick nap. Remington exited the bathroom with just a towel wrapped around his waist and joined me on the bed. I wasn't asleep just yet.

"Hey, are you okay?"

"Yes, I'm fine. I'm just a little tired. I need a quick nap."

"Fine, I'll lay here with you until you fall asleep babe." He kissed me gently on my forehead.

I didn't respond. I just closed my eyes and prayed for sleep to find me quickly and it did. I woke up to Alivia gently shaking me.

"Lexie, Dad wants you to come downstairs to meet Grandma and Grandpa."

"Oh my goodness, what time is it? How long have I been asleep?"

"You've been asleep a really long time but Dad wouldn't let us wake you up."

"Okay, baby. I'll be downstairs in just a few minutes. Will you go ask your dad to come here, please?"

"Okay."

Alivia left the room as I got up and grabbed my phone. It was almost eight o'clock. Why would Remington let me sleep so damn long? Ugh, now all the attention will be on me when I enter the room. Remington burst through the room being his usually playful self.

"Why did you let me sleep so long? It's almost bedtime."

"You were obviously tired. Plus, you needed your rest because I doubt we'll get any sleep tonight."

"Remington, I'm not having sex with your parents in the house."

"Why not? You don't think my pops will be sexing my mom down the hall. Well, I'm here to tell you that he will."

"How long have they been here?"

"Only like an hour or so. David and Anthony are here as well so you can meet everyone."

"Umm, okay."

"Lexie, there's no need to be nervous. They are going to love you. Not the way I love you, but they will love you nonetheless."

Again, I didn't say anything at the mention of the L word. I'm not sure what made me so nervous or apprehensive about him using it but I was. There was no doubt that I loved Remington. I knew that long before now. Hearing him profess his love to me literally made my stomach knot. Loving Remington was no easy task and admitting to him that I love him would undoubtedly take my anxiety to a new level. There were still so many unknowns about him. Most of the time, I felt like I was dealing with two different people and it gave me pause.

I hurriedly moved about, making sure I looked halfway decent before going downstairs to meet the rest of Remington's immediate family. He grabbed me by the waist.

"Calm down. They are just regular folks. No big deal."

I smiled and put on my best game face and we headed downstairs. The group was engaged in conversation but as soon as we entered the room they all grew quiet. Santoria was the first to break the silence.

"We thought y'all were up there going half on a baby again."

If I wasn't so brown skinned my face would have been flushed pink. I was a deer in headlights. The rest of the room burst into laughter, including Remington. I didn't find it funny that we were the center of the joke.

"Mom, Dad, David and Anthony, this is Alexis. Alexis this is my dad, mom, and brothers-in-law, David and Anthony."

I extended my hand to his dad first and he dismissed it before pulling me in for a hug. I was a little caught off guard.

"We hug in this family," Mrs. Slayton said.

I then hugged his mom and the two brothers-in-law. I took a seat on the sectional with Santoria and Synthia. The kids were still up with the exception of DJ and Amir.

Remington sat down beside me, leaned in, and whispered in my ear, "See, that wasn't bad. Loosen up unless you want to relieve more stress right now."

"Remington, let Lexie breathe. She is fine," Synthia said.

"I know. I'm just trying to get her to loosen up and let the nervousness go."

I looked at him and rolled my eyes. Nothing is a damn secret with him. It seemed his whole family operated that way.

"Do you want to sit on the back porch with us? The guys are about to start grilling. Well, really Dad because we know he's not about to let anyone else grill," Santoria said.

"Sure, I'll be out in just a moment. I'm going to get something to drink first."

I went into the kitchen to see Remington's mom cutting up strawberries and mangoes for mixed drinks. I noticed that she gave me the same stare down that her daughters had given me, except it was more intense. I returned the favor. She smiled and winked. I couldn't help but think this whole damn family is crazy.

"So Alexis, tell me about yourself."

"Umm, I'm from Tennessee, no children, I'm a consultant by day but I'm getting ready to release a book soon. That's pretty much it."

"So, you don't have hobbies or anything interesting going on?"

"Well, of course. I like taking vacations, running, yoga, writing, reading, and cooking."

"Oh, you can cook?"

"Umm, yes ma'am."

"Most young girls can't cook these days. I'm happy I taught my girls how to cook."

I didn't say anything because I really wasn't feeling the vibe from Mrs. Slayton.
Thankfully,
Remington entered the kitchen to ask about drinks. I grabbed a bottle of water out of the refrigerator and headed to the back yard with his sisters. I'll leave him be with his mom.

When I stepped out the front door I noticed Santoria and her husband, David, in what seemed to be a heated discussion. I averted my eyes quickly as I didn't not want to appear to be eavesdropping. I finally found a spot farther away from them and took a much needed seat. If I was being honest with myself, I was still reeling and tired from my Remington experience earlier. Each time I was with Remington sexually, intimately, or in general it is an experience. Today seemed like it was a lot more than that. I was going to need time to process it all.

The backdoor opened and I saw his big, bright smile. It hasn't been too many times I didn't see Remington smiling. He seemed to be even more excited and happy today. Maybe this is how he acts when he's around his family. Santoria and David were still having their conversation. Synthia came out not long after Remington. She flounced over to me and took the chair next to me. Remington stood closer to the backdoor, observing. I'm pretty sure he was eavesdropping on his sister and brother-in-law's conversation. Rude ass.

Synthia interrupted my thoughts.

"How do you put up with Remington and his foolishness?"

I chuckled lightly. "I have no idea how or why I continue to put up with his mess."

"You're better than me. He's always been the same Remington ever since I can remember. I can't say that's good or bad. I just know it's consistent."

"Yeah, I'm not sure if that's good or bad either."

"I think my parents knew he would be a handful," she said.

"Why you say that?"

"They named him Remington. After the firearms. That's a problem within itself."

"I wondered about the story behind his name. It's so cool."

"My dad is a lover of firearms and it didn't help that he's originally from Huntsville, AL where Remington Firearms headquarters were."

"Wow, that's interesting. I'm surprised your mom was okay with your dad naming him Remington."

"Girl, I imagine back then my mom would've let me my dad name him anything. She's always been crazy in love with Dad."

"Awe, that's cute."

"Yeah, sometimes and other times it's sickening. They still act like high school lovers."

"That says a lot about them," I said. "How long have they been married?"

"Almost forty years. It's a blessing and a curse."

"I can imagine."

There was an awkward silence for just a brief moment. Remington finally made his way to where Synthia and I were sitting.

"I hate to interrupt your girl talk but Synthia, come have a word with me."

"I guess please would be a stretch. Remington right now I just want to enjoy Alexis and this nice weather."

"It will only take a second. I promise."

Reluctantly, Synthia got up from her seat and they walked far enough to be out of listening range for me. I really felt like I was interrupting everyone's private conversations. Santoria and David in one corner of the yard whispering and Remington and Synthia in the other corner doing the same thing. Ugh, I could've stayed asleep.

Surprisingly, Remington and Synthia were not long but I could tell the mood had changed for Synthia. Santoria finally joined Remington, Synthia, and I. David headed in the house to do some work, but Santoria didn't seem too happy about that. I wonder if he worked long hours like Remington. If so, I know that can be frustrating, especially with three children at home. Remington sat in my chair and I sat in his lap. I'm sure this was a bad decision.

Synthia's husband, Anthony, and their parents joined us outside. We all sat and talked about a lot of nothing for quite a while. I wasn't tired but the introvert in me was screaming for her time.

"As much fun as it has been, I'm going to call it a night."

"Going to bed so early?" Mr. Slayton asked.

"Yes, I'm tired and I know I'll need to be up early to make some phone calls and get a few things done."

"Oh, you're a workaholic, too?" Mrs. Slayton asked.

"No, not at all. I just have a few calls to make so I won't be too behind when I get back to work. Good night everyone."

I leaned in and dusted a light kiss on Remington's lips. Of course, he decided to do something extra like quickly swipe his tongue across my bottom lip. Instantly, my body temperature rose three degrees. I was such a loss cause when it came to him. I got off his lap and headed into the house. I made my way upstairs to our sleeping quarters, took a hot shower, and dressed for bed. I had just pulled my journal out when Remington entered the room. Lord, I just need fifteen more minutes to myself.

"Hey, I just wanted to make sure you were okay."

"I'm fine. I've showered and now I'm going to write in my journal before I close my eyes for the night."

"Oh okay. Are you sure you are okay?"

"Yes, Remington. Why wouldn't I be?"

"Umm, today has been a lot. A lot was said and you've seemed off ever since."

"I'm just tired. Long day traveling. I need to get some rest."

"Okay, I'm heading back downstairs with my folks unless you want me to stay here with you."

"No, go enjoy your family. I'll be sleep in no time."

"I'm waking that ass up when I get back. So, get some rest."

I didn't say anything as Remington left the room. I started what was supposed to be a short journal post but it turned into this four page letter. I didn't realize how much I needed to get out of my system. I finally finished my post, put my journal back in my bag, and got comfortable in bed. I'm sure I was asleep in less than five minutes.

I was awakened by the sound of a hushed voice. I looked at my phone to see it was 2:48 AM. Remington was in the restroom talking to someone on the phone but I couldn't make out what he was saying. He emerged from the restroom about ten minutes after I woke up.

"Who were you talking to this late? Is everything okay?"

"I thought you were asleep. Did I wake you?"

"No. Who were you talking to this late?"

"It's not important. Work stuff that should've been handled earlier today."

"It couldn't wait until tomorrow morning? Sounds pretty important and urgent."

I turned my back to Remington as he stood in the door of the restroom with nothing on. This man had no problem walking around butt naked all the time. I was not going to be distracted by his gorgeous body and infectious smile. I just found it weird that work calls would get answered this time of the morning while on vacation. If the building wasn't burning down, he shouldn't be receiving phone calls.

Remington joined me in bed. He tried to cozy up but my mood was killed. I wasn't up for sex or anything else. I turned to face the opposite direction.

"Come on, Lexie. Don't act like that."

"I'm not acting like anything. I'm tired and really need to get back to sleep."

"Fine. Good night, babe."

"Good night, Remington."

The rest of the weekend with Remington's family was fun and a lot less awkward. Besides Remington's mom being sarcastic from time to time, all was well with the rest of the trip. I did notice that Santoria and her husband intentionally stayed away from her mom whenever possible. With all the fun we had, I was so excited to get back to Georgia on Sunday afternoon. When we made it to the airport I caught an uber home and Remington headed to meet the girls' mom at the halfway point to Charlotte, NC. Honestly, I was thankful for the alone time.

I loved being with Remington and the girls but Remington could be overwhelming. After spending days with his family, him confessing his love for me, and me trying to work through all my emotions, I welcomed the time alone. Even if it were just for one night. I needed to be able to process what I felt and strategize how to best handle my emotions. This would not be an easy task because I was already emotionally attached to Remington. It was easy to love him, especially the Remington I got while on vacation. He was attentive, affectionate, intimate, caring, and most importantly, present.

Perhaps, it was just best for me to throw caution to the wind and see where this journey with Remington led.

The next nine months were the same for Remington and I. We spent more and more time together and I love you became a common phrase for both of us. I spent more time at his house than I did at my own. I think I was more excited about the weekends that girls visited that Remington. I was so in love with the twins. They were the sweetest and we always had a blast when we were together.

One weekend the twins were in town and we were curled up on the couch doing what loved to do, watch Disney movies. Alivia was laying in my lap and Reagan was snuggled on my other side.

Randomly, Alivia said, "Lexie I think you are so cool."

Before I could even respond, Reagan chimed in, "Me too. And I miss you when we are at our mom's house."

"Awe, I think you are the coolest twins ever."

"And you always buy us stuff. Lots of stuff," Reagan said.

"More stuff than daddy," Alivia giggled.

"That's because I'm a better shopper than your dad."

"Daddy hates shopping," Alivia said while making this exaggerated face.

"Yes, he does."

"We love hanging out with you doing fun, girly stuff," Reagan said.

"Awe, I love you two."

"We love you, too, Lexie," they simultaneously said.

Alivia reached and hugged my waist while Reagan hugged my neck. I didn't say anything for a few minutes. I just sat and reflected on the brief interaction with the girls. When they were here in Georgia they were my girls. I spent the most time with them. Like now, Remington was still working long hours which was fine with me because I enjoyed the quality time the twins and I spent together.

I successfully released my first book and hosted book signings in different cities. I was so excited anytime someone from a book club asked me to be their guest. While we both seemed to have less time, Remington and I made sure to spend whatever free time we had together. There was such a peace between the two of us. I was in a really happy place. We even started having conversations about our future. I would be lying if I said I wasn't over the moon excited.

The Scandal – Sex

Remington and I had been dating for a little over two years. It was a few months before Thanksgiving. It was one of the rare occasions that we were at my house. Remington had us watching another one of his "must see" docuseries. I had just entered the living room from pouring two glasses of wine. I settled back on the couch and rested my head on his chest and closed my eyes. I knew it would only be a matter of minutes after I finished my wine that I would be asleep. I relished in the comfort of laying against Remington's chest. It was a rare occasion that he wasn't working from his phone.

"Lexie, what are you doing for Thanksgiving this year?"

"My family hasn't decided who's hosting dinner this year. What are your plans?"

"Let's host both of our families. We can host it at your house but it'll be good to have both our families in one place."

"Are you sure? That's a lot of people."

"Yeah, my folks can stay at my house and your folks can stay at your house. Or anyone who wants to get a hotel can get a hotel or do AirBnB."

"Umm, okay. I'll check to see if my family would like to come to Georgia then."

"Let me know if I need to help you out with persuasion. You know I have a skillset."

Remington smiled and ran his tongue across his bottom lip. I instantly recognized the game he was attempting to play. He knew that small things like that would ignite a need in me that only he could satisfy. We briefly discussed Thanksgiving dinner and the possibility of hosting it.

"It's getting late. I'm heading to bed. I have an early morning."

"I'll join you in about an hour," Remington said.

"Oh, you're working late?" I'm sure he could hear the disappointment in my voice.

"I just need to finish up a couple things and then I'll be to bed. I'll wake you when I get there."

"Whatever."

I got in bed and was asleep before I could give any more thought to anything. When I rolled over to look at my phone it was 2:34 AM. Remington was still not in bed. He must have fallen asleep downstairs.

I headed downstairs and I noticed he was still awake, texting on his phone.

"I thought you had fallen asleep down here but you're still up."

"Sorry, I got to watching a few episodes of this show and lost track of time. I'm headed up now."

He got up from the couch and headed upstairs but I noticed he left his phone. I followed upstairs to the bedroom and we fell asleep. No sex. No cuddling. Nothing.

I tried not to give too much thought to it during the day but it didn't really sit well with me. After work, I decided that I was staying home tonight. I needed a few days to myself in my space to get myself together. I just knew it would be an all out fight with Remington when I told him I was staying home for a couple days, but surprisingly he was cool with it.

We spoke briefly on Monday night. Since I was inundated with work, I stayed up late both Monday and Tuesday. Wednesday morning I felt refreshed and well rested. Remington text that morning asking if we could have dinner around 7 PM. Of course, I agreed. At this point, I missed him. My workday was hectic. When I looked up it was 6:15. Shit. I needed to get a move on. I wanted to change clothes but I didn't have time to go home, change clothes, and then make it to the restaurant in time. Guess, I'll be wearing my work clothes.

I made it to the restaurant at a little after seven o'clock. I was literally fifteen minutes away from the restaurant but Atlanta's traffic was always so horrid. I walked in and spotted Remington immediately. He must have felt my presence because he turned instantly.

He stood and gave me a quick kiss on the lips.

"Bad traffic?"

"Yes, it's horrible. Plus, I lost track of time working."

"Work has been busy, huh?"

"A little more than usual."

The waiter appeared with our drinks.

"Great, thanks."

The waiter stood there awkwardly waiting for us to place an order. I'm not sure why he just didn't ask if we were ready. My phone started ringing and I reached into my bag to grab it.

"Do you know what you want?"

"Yes, my usual. I need to take this call really quickly." I stepped away from the table to answer my phone. It was my dad who never called during the week. "Hi, Dad!"

"Hey, Alexis. I'm calling to let you know your uncle passed a couple of hours ago."

"Oh no! I'm so sorry. Are Grandma and Grandpa okay? Are you okay?"

"We are as well as to be expected. I'm calling you and your siblings so y'all will know. I'm headed to Mom and Dad's house soon."

"How is Aunt Melanie? Is she okay?"

"I haven't spoken with her but I can imagine not. It wasn't unexpected but it's still hard to process. I'll call you when I make it to your grandparents' house."

"Okay, dad. Thanks for letting me know. I'll be making arrangements to be home in the next day or so. Talk to you soon. Love you."

"I love you, too, Alexis."

I took a few moments to gather my thoughts before I headed back to the dinner table. The very short walk seemed to take forever. When I made it back to the table Remington was texting on his phone.

"Is everything okay, Lexie?"

"No, my uncle passed a couple of hours ago. That was my dad calling to let me know."

Remington reached his hand across the table. "I'm sorry, babe. Are you okay? Can I do something?"

"No, I'm fine. Let's just eat dinner."

Remington and I made small talk as we ate dinner. He talked about an upcoming project that he was excited about. Most of the time my thoughts were on my grandparents and my Aunt Melanie. I can't imagine what she must be going through.

"When do you plan to head home?"

"I'll probably go tomorrow afternoon or either Thursday morning. I'm not sure yet. Depends on how I feel."

"I think you should fly as opposed to drive."

"You know I'm not flying when I can make the six-hour drive with my eyes closed. Plus, a last minute flight will be unnecessarily expensive."

"Just a thought. Are you staying home tonight or my house?"

"Home. You can come by if you want. I need to pack a bag and be prepared to leave."

"I'll come by after I go home first."

We finished dinner and we both headed to our respective homes. It was a little after nine o'clock when I made it home and started packing clothes. I wasn't sure how long I would be gone but I was thankful for the ability to work from home. After I packed clothes, I started to look at work emails and cancel appointments for the upcoming week. Soon, I realized it was well after eleven o'clock. I text Remington.

Alexis: What time are you getting here?

I didn't receive an immediate response. I waited for about fifteen minutes before I called. No answer. His phone actually rang once and went to voicemail. I was too tired to even care at this point. I showered and crawled into bed. Of course, I didn't fall right to sleep. Remington is such an asshole. I grabbed my phone and decided to send him a long ass text message.

Alexis: A phone call would have been nice. You and your disappearing acts are not cool. They are not cool at any time but especially tonight. You don't know if I needed you emotionally or not. It's very inconsiderate. I'll talk to you when I get back from Tennessee and not a day before then. I need to focus on my family and myself.

I hit send and rolled over to count sheep as I prayed that sleep would find me soon. I dozed off but was awakened to the sound of my garage opening. I looked at my phone and it was 4:33 AM. The motherfucking nerve of him. I sat up in my bed waiting on his ass to come into my bedroom.

Remington entered my bedroom, shocked to see me wide awake.

"I bet you did. Why? Because it's 4:30 in the morning and you are just getting here?"

"Lexie, it's late. I lost track of time."

"Really, Remington, that's your excuse? You could have stayed home or wherever you were as opposed to coming to my damn house this time of the morning. You know I have a job to go to in a couple of hours."

"Lex, come on. You're overreacting. I lost track of time but I wanted to come be with you."

"You shouldn't have."

I snatched the covers up and laid down. I was not in the mood for his bullshit this morning. I had my alarm set for six o'clock. I would work until 11:30 and then get on the road to go home.

"Forgive me, Lexie. I have a lot going on right now."

"We both do."

That was the last thing I said to him. I knew I wasn't going to sleep but I didn't want to engage in any type of conversation with him. He didn't attempt to talk or touch me either.

When my alarm went off I jumped out of bed, got dressed, quickly made breakfast, and loaded my bags in the car. By the time Remington made it downstairs, I was headed out the door.

"Lock the door and set the alarm when you leave. Thanks."

"Alexis, come on. You're just leaving like that? You're going to be away at least a week. Let's not leave on these terms."

"That wasn't a concern of yours last night. I'm not sure what has changed this morning."

"Alexis Carter. You are being inconsiderate. I have a lot going on and I just lost track of time."

"You have a lot going on? Everyone in the fucking world has a lot going on but we prioritize and I see I'm not at the top of your list even when I'm dealing with a family death. So yea, I'm not happy with you right now. Now, excuse me while I head to work."

"Lexie, call me when you get to work. Let's talk."

I didn't bother responding and I didn't plan to call. I drove to work in silence. I was furious with Remington. It was clear that something was off with him but I wasn't going digging to see what that something was. Getting to work was a nightmare. It just added to my already frustrating morning. I finally made it to the parking garage after being in bumper to bumper traffic for more than an hour. The best thing about long car rides is my ability to sort through all the thoughts.

I made it into the office and headed straight to my first meeting. I dreaded this meeting but I also knew the quicker it was over, the faster I could get on the road and head to Tennessee to be with my folks.

The client meeting lasted way longer than I expected. Remington called twice and sent several text messages while I was in the meeting. I didn't bother reading them. I wasn't ready to talk with him yet. When my meeting finally ended it was a little after noon. I had one more task that I needed to complete before I could head out for the rest of the week. I didn't even bother going to my desk. I stayed in the conference room and completed the last request for a client's report.

While I finished up my last task, Remington called again. I decided to put him out of his misery and answer the damn phone.

"Yes, Remington."

"Alexis, come on. I think you are overreacting."

"Okay, tell me something you haven't already said. Tell me what you were doing that was so important that you couldn't make it to your girlfriend until four thirty in the morning?"

"I told you, I lost track of time."

"Oh, that's the only explanation that you have?"

"It's the only one I need."

Apparently. Look, I'm working. What do you want?"

"Can we have lunch before you leave for Tennessee?"

"No, I'm already late getting on the road. I don't want to get home too late."

"Okay, when are you getting back in town?"

"I'm not sure Remington, why?"

"Because I'm your boyfriend and need to know this."

"Funny how you only remember that when it's convenient for you. I will call you once I get on the road. I need to finish up here with no distraction."

"Make sure you call me. Bye, babe."

"Bye, Remington."

I ended the phone conversation with Remington and grabbed my things to head out of the door. As I was leaving out, my text notification dinged and I looked to see it was text from Nikki. I checked it quickly.

Nicole Wright: I asked Remington about you last night. I'm sorry to hear about your uncle. Sending my condolences.

My stomach turned after reading her message. Why was Remington with Nicole last night? I thought he had cut off all communication with her. I decided not to respond right away to Nicole but I was going to ask Remington what the hell was he doing with her. Where did she see him? Did they go to an event? What the fuck?

When I made it to my car I responded to Nicole's text message.

Alexis: Thanks for the condolences. Saw Remington where? I hope you are doing well.

Nicole didn't respond immediately but I knew something wasn't right with the situation. My stomach was literally in knots. I decided to call Remington. He answered on the third ring sounding breathless.

"Hey Lexie. Are you on the road?"

I decided to skip all the pleasantries and get straight to the point.

"Where were you last night that you saw Nicole?"

"Huh, what?"

"Nicole texted me and said she saw you last night. Where were you that she saw you?"

"Antonio and I had to finish a project that the three of us were working on so we met at the office to finish up."

"Oh, so that's what you were doing when you lost track of time?"

"Yes, Alexis."

"Remington, something is not right about this situation."

"Nikki is crazy and messy. I'm not sure why she felt the need to text and tell you that."

"Well, I guess she was sending her condolences. So, this project couldn't wait until today?"

"Alexis, no. I have a business to run and sometimes it requires long, late hours. You knew that when we started dating!"

"First off, don't raise your voice at me. Secondly, you need to learn how to prioritize. Third, until I become a priority for you let's just not communicate. I'll let you sort through all that you have going on and I'll…"

"Again, you are overreacting. It was a last minute thing that needed to be handled.

Damn, I don't know how else to explain this shit to you."

"You don't owe me an explanation. Bye Remington."

I hung up the phone. I was so pissed off that my hands were visibly shaking. A small pool of sweat gathered on my nose as it often did when I was angry. In addition to that, my right jaw was twitching. I don't think I had ever been so upset at Remington. The nerve of him to raise his damn voice like I'm being petty about last night.

I turned on my positive affirmations, sent a text to my folks to let them know I was finally on the road, and mentally prepared to fight Atlanta traffic. There was always traffic in Atlanta regardless of the time of day. I needed this seven-hour drive to clear my head and sort through all of my emotions.

After driving for three hours, I stopped right outside of Birmingham to get gas and snacks for the rest of my drive. Snacks were my go to when my emotions were all over the place and they were definitely all over the place. I finally checked my phone once inside the gas station. Remington had text and I had several texts from my siblings letting me know that we were going to meet at my grandparents' home.

I responded "Sure" to Remington's text asking me to let him know when I made it home.

The rest of the drive home was entertaining. I did a conference call with Brooklyn and Reign. I didn't mention anything about Remington to them because I was not in the mood for advice and what not. We talked about everything and decided we needed to link up once and I got back in town. We would surprise Justice with lunch or something. I can imagine she was overwhelmed with the twins.

The thought of Justice happily married with her family brought a somber mood over me. While I am happy for Justice and Corey, I wondered when my time would come. I thought Remington was my person but from the way he's been moving lately I'm not so sure of that. Last night was just one instance in which his actions were not aligned with what he said.

Brooklyn, Reign, and I ended our conversation when I was twenty minutes from my grandparents' home. I'd never been so happy to be back home but definitely sad that it was under these circumstances. When I turned on the street I was met with a line of cars. All my folks were here for sure. I parked my car, grabbed my phone and purse, and headed down the street. I was spotted by my oldest brother and two of my nieces. My nieces took off running, obviously racing to see who could get to me the fastest. They almost knocked me down. This is what I missed the most.

I spent the next few days hanging out with my family and preparing to lay my uncle to rest. Remington and I didn't really talk much. I tried calling him on FaceTime a few times in the evenings or at night but he would text that he was working. Then he would try to FaceTime me during the day but I was busy with being an aunt, helping my grandparents out, or doing some work for clients. I guess our schedules didn't mesh.

After being home for nine days, it was time for me to make my way back to Atlanta. As much as I loved being home, I couldn't wait to get back to my space with lots of peace and quiet. I text Remington to let him know I would be home later that evening. His response was, "Okay, see you then." I also text Brooklyn and Reign as well. The drive back to Atlanta didn't seem as daunting. Mostly because I was so ready to be back home and if I'm being honest, I wanted to see Remington.

When I made it home, Remington's vehicle was parked in my driveway. Hmm, I wonder why he didn't park in the garage? I let up the garage, parked my car, and went inside. I decided to leave unloading my bags for later. When I walked in I smelled food. It smelled delicious.

"Remington!" I yelled.

"Hey babe, I'm in the kitchen."

I walked into the kitchen and my breath caught in my throat. Remington had nicely decorated the adjoining dining room with what had to be at least twelve dozens of roses. Not just red roses but white and yellow as well. Candles were lit and there was wine. Not his fancy kind of wine but my favorite, Rosetta Black Wine.

"Umm, what's going on?"

"Lexie, I know I messed up. I want you to know you are a priority for me."

"I appreciate the food. Although, I can tell by the packaging that you did not cook it. It's the thought that counts."

"I figured I would order from one of your favorite restaurants and not mess up one of your favorite meals."

"I love the flowers. I'm sure you spent way too much but they are gorgeous."

"You deserve the flowers and more. And there is more but I want you to get comfortable and ready to eat first."

"Yeah, I need to shower and get into something more comfortable."

"Yes, you do. I'll grab your bags out of the car and bring them upstairs while you shower."

My heart was pounding as I took the stairs two at a time. I thought I was in awe when I walked into the kitchen just a few moments ago but my heart stopped when I made it to my bedroom. There were sunflowers all over the room. Remington knows I love sunflowers. If this wasn't an apology I don't know what is.

Looking around the room, my eyes began to water. I think he's trying to get me to understand that I am a priority in his life. Something sparkling on the bed caught my attention. I was so overwhelmed by the sight of the sunflowers that I didn't notice the black sequin dress laid across the bed with a note laying on top. I picked up the small card and read it out loud:

Alexis, you are a priority in my life. I know I messed up but a lot of this is new for me. I love you and want to make it up to you. Have dinner with me. Please wear this dress and the new fun items you will find in the bathroom.

It wasn't until after I had finished reading the card that I noticed a pair of matching heels laying on the floor in front of the dress. The dress was floor length and strapless with an amazing split. I couldn't wait to put it on. I headed into the bathroom where I found a new strapless black lace bra and thong. I would probably skip the thong and just go commando. I hopped in the shower and enjoyed the warmth of the water as it ran down my back. I inhaled the magical scent of my aromatherapy body wash and relaxed into the water. My mind reeled over the time and effort Remington had put into apologizing for his actions. I wondered what else he had planned for the night. I needed a few more seconds before I walked back into Remington's world. It could be overwhelming in good and bad ways. Tonight was overwhelming in the best way possible.

When I exited the shower I heard jazz playing from downstairs. I took my time drying off and moisturizing my body. Once I completed that task, I put on one of my favorite perfumes, Candy by Prada. I put on my lace bra and threw on my bathroom as I finished getting ready. My hair was in its natural state so I didn't have much to do. My twist out was still fresh and cute. Thank God! I did my face with a light brushing of makeup, brow fill-in, eyeliner, mascara, and a smokey eye look. I then pulled out my tear drop diamond earrings and necklace to match. Finally, I put on the dress Remington had laid out for me. It was a perfect fit. I slid on the Bebe heels. After one final glance at myself in the mirror, I headed downstairs to partake in what was sure to be an excellent meal.

When I made it downstairs I was shocked to see Remington dressed in a black tuxedo. The table was set. He was leaning against the island sipping his wine. He looked just as sinfully delicious as he did the first night I laid eyes on him. He had that charming smile plastered on his face. Irresistible. He slowly made his way to me and I was mesmerized by his every move. I watched in awe as he effortlessly turned me on without touching me. This was the

Remington that I had come to know and love. Thank God, he was back.

Remington pulled out my chair and beckoned for me to have a seat. I complied. He moved across the table and took his seat. I expected an awkward silence but there was none. Remington jumped right into conversation.

"Alexis, I know I was an asshole. Please forgive me."

"Remington, you are forgiven but you have to work on your communication. All this could have been avoided if you would have simply said you needed to work on a project but to not answer my phone calls or respond to text messages is unacceptable."

"You're right. I'm sorry baby. I won't let that happen again. I also want to address something else."

"Umm, okay. What?"

"You are a priority in my life. I don't always get it right but I hope tonight shows that you are and I have no intentions of letting that change."

"I get it. I'll try to be more understanding of your demanding work schedule, too."

"I would appreciate that."

The rest of the time we spent eating and making small talk. He asked about my trip home and I gave him most of the details. Just as we were finishing up dinner there was a knock on the door. Puzzled, I looked at Remington.

"I'm not sure who that could be but let me get the door."

"No, I got it. You can go ahead and clear the table."

"Okay."

I grabbed the dinner plates first and headed to the kitchen sink. I couldn't see who was at the door but I heard voices so it was more than one person. Remington walked into the kitchen just as I finished clearing the table.

"I have one more surprise for you."

Remington looked nervous which was out of character for him. I can't remember a time when he was flustered or nervous about anything.

"Okay." I gave him a puzzled look.

"Follow me into the conversation room."

I did as he asked. When I walked into the room there were roses all over the place.

The roses in this room were only red. There were so many of them. I also noticed two guys standing in the room off to the side in the corners. One guy had his camera and the other had a video camera.

"What's going on?" I stammered over my words.

"Alexis, you are one of the most important people in my life. These last nine days have been hell without you here with me. I don't want to experience that ever again. Will you do me the honor of being my wife?"

I was in such shock that it took me a few seconds too long to respond. Remington cleared his throat to get my attention.

"YES! Yes, Remington."

This was the last thing I was expecting after returning from Tennessee, especially since we had left on such bad terms. I couldn't think of a better way for a proposal to go. There was so much thought and effort put into tonight's proposal. I was over the moon excited and I had a million and one things running through my head. I wanted to enjoy the moment but my brain was working overtime. I needed to call my parents and siblings. Damn, I needed to call Brooklyn and Reign. Oh my goodness! I'm getting married to my person. God hears and answers prayers. There was so much that needed to be discussed.

Remington sat in silence and stared at me. At least, I think he was staring at me. Maybe he was staring past me into space.

"You should take tomorrow off and we can just chill and enjoy our moment."

"Remington, I've been off long enough. Not that I didn't do work while I was home."

"My point exactly. Just take a real day off and relax. Let's stay in our bubble a little longer."

"I'll work from home the first part of the morning and then after noon I'm all yours. I just need to respond to a few emails."

"Okay, Lexie. But you shouldn't complain about me always working."

"Well, I had planned to respond to the emails tonight but my fiancé had other plans."

"Oh, I like how that sounds coming off your sexy lips. Let's see how we can close the night with a bang. Tell me what's next."

"I'll show you why you just made the best decision of your life by choosing me as your fiancé."

"Oh really? Well, show me baby."

Slowly I stood and Remington joined me. I had one simple question for him. "Here or the bedroom?"

"Oh baby, I can't wait until we get to the bedroom."

That was all the confirmation I needed. I put on a show for Remington. I swayed my hips with sensual movement as I slowly began to undress. Well, it didn't take long since I had on a dress but Remington was not prepared for what was under the dress or lack thereof. I heard a small growl escape his lips when he realized I didn't bother with the thong he laid out for me.

"Come here, you naughty girl. You didn't like the thong daddy laid out for you?"

"Not with this dress."

"Oh, I see. My Lexie."

Remington unhooked my bra and let it drop to the floor. I stood in front of him naked with nothing but my heels on. He placed wet kisses on my neck and I was instantly turned on. So much so that I could smell my own sex. Remington ran his masculine hands down my spine. He let his left hand settle at the small of my back and used his right hand to pinch my nipples repeatedly. I was so turned on by both of these actions that I couldn't contain the moan that escaped my lips. I wanted him in the worst possible way.

"Baby, I want you."

"Oh, do you now? How bad?"

"Really bad. I need to feel you inside of me."

"I know babe. Your body always lets me know when you need me."

Remington removed his right hand from my left nipple but kept his left hand at the small of my back. He guided me to the couch and commanded that I sit with my legs wide open. I complied. He dropped to his knees and placed small, wet kisses on my breast making a trail to my navel.

"Lay down, Lexie."

Again, I complied. Remington ran his index finger between the folds of my sex. I didn't recognize my own voice when the shriek left my mouth. My sex was so sensitive. Any small touch or lick would most likely send me into an orgasmic state and Remington knew this. He knew my body well.

"I like how you are always ready for me. You're so wet, baby."

"I know. I want you now."

"I know you do. But you have to wait just a little longer. You don't come until I say come. Understood?"

Umm, yeah. I didn't really think it was possible to hold off from coming but I would try.

Remington continued his game of foreplay. He placed kisses all over my body, including around my vagina but he never actually kissed me there. It was torture to say the least. Finally, he slipped two fingers inside me while he whispered all the things he wanted to do to me. I was so close to coming and just as my orgasm was building he removed his fingers.

"You don't cum until I say so. Understood?"

"Remington, I need to cum."

"When I say so."

He slipped his two fingers back inside of me and began to work at a steady rhythm. He slowly began to make his way off his knees and used his tongue to trace different patterns on my stomach and chest. All the while, he kept his fingers inside of me. I was becoming more and more sensitive with each stroke and lick of his tongue. His lips finally reached mine and he removed his fingers. The hunger I felt for him was unbelievable. I devoured his mouth. Remington pulled back.

"What? What's wrong?"

"I need to undress before I burst through my suit, baby."

"Oh! Well, hurry."

Remington made quick work of his fingers and undressed. This chocolate god stood before me stark naked and I could claim him as mine. I couldn't contain the grin that spread across my face while I watched in awe of his chiseled body.

"Like what you see, baby girl?"

"Maybe."

"Oh no, you don't get to be coy with me. Do you like what you see?"

"No, I love what I see. I love how chiseled your chest and arms are. I love how your ass is perfect and muscular. I love how your penis stands at attention for me. I love what your fingers do to me. I love how your lips feel on every inch of my body."

"Oh, baby. I like that. You should talk to daddy like that more often."

Remington slowly slid his penis inside of me. It was the best feeling of the night. He began to move painstakingly slow but eventually increased his speed. I met his thrusts with my own. He leaned in and bit my nipples, followed by soft kisses. The contrast of his actions was amazing. I was losing my mind. His thrusts became harder and harder. I was so ready to cum. I'm not sure where my head was but before I could even think about it I asked, "Daddy, can I cum now?"

"Yes, baby. Cum for me."

And just like that we both came together. It was the best feeling in the world. I was on cloud nine and couldn't come down even if I wanted to. Today was the best day ever. I was exhausted from the long drive and the overwhelming happiness that I felt with my new fiancé.

The next morning, I called my parents and siblings to let them know about the engagement. My parents were happy as long as I was happy. My sister had plenty of questions and wanted a play by play as to how it all happened. Everyone was excited as long as I was excited. I knew my next phone calls would be a lot different. I needed to call Brooklyn and Reign. I had to mentally prepare for the onslaught of questions.

Remington was in my office working and I was still in bed. I sent a quick text to our group chat.

Alexis: Let's conference call today. We need to catch up.

Reign: I'm free pretty much anytime.

Brooklyn didn't respond right away so I decided to get up and start breakfast.

"Good morning, my love."

"Good morning, Remington. You're up working when I thought we were staying in bed most of the day."

"I needed to get some things out of the way early today so you can have my undivided attention."

"Oh really? Well, I'm making breakfast. Any requests?"

"French toast, bacon, eggs, and fresh fruit."

"Well damn! That's an IHOP order but I'll see if I have ingredients for French toast."

"Great, I'll be down in a few."

I made my way into the kitchen and pulled out the ingredients for breakfast. I hadn't eaten pork in years, but I always kept some at my house for Remington. My phone dinged and I checked the messages. Brooklyn finally responded that she was free for the next hour.

I decided to call while I was making breakfast. I called Reign first.

"Hey, Reign."

"Hey, Lexie."

"Girl, let's get Brooke on the phone while she has time to talk to us."

"I'll conference her in."

Reign called Brooke and she finally answered on the third ring.

"Damn, I didn't think you were going to answer," I said.

"Well, if my damn purse wasn't so junky, I would've been able to find my damn phone."

"So, what's up?" Reign asked.

"Umm, Remington proposed last night."

"What?" Both Brooke and Reign yelled, simultaneously.

"Yes, last night and it was amazing. I mean so damn amazing."

"Why didn't you tell us this last night? We could've had the wedding planned by now," Reign joked.

"Okay we need all the details and don't leave anything out. OMG, Lexie!" Brooklyn yelled.

"Well, when I got back from Tennessee he had dinner delivered and apologized for being an asshole before I left. He had the house filled with all these roses and sunflowers. He requested that I get dressed for dinner. When I went upstairs to my room I found a new dress, shoes, panties, and bra. Like he put so much thought into it."

"Damn, Lexie. That sounds romantic," Reign said.

"Sounds romantic. Reign please. It is romantic. Okay, what else happened?" Brooke asked.

"After dinner there was a knock on the door. Remington went to the door while I continued to clear the table. I heard him talking to someone when I went into the conversation room."

"Who the hell was at the door? What time of the night was it? You never have company." Brooke stated the obvious.

"Well, it was the photographer and videographer that Remington hired to capture the moment. I walked into the conversation room, looking puzzled. Before I could figure out what was happening, Remington was on one knee proposing. He proposed y'all. Like I'm marrying the man of my dreams."

"Okay, did you cry or were you nervous, excited? We need to know your emotions in that moment," Reign demanded.

"I was more shocked than anything. I was like, what is happening? After the initial shock I was so excited. I was like wow, especially since we were not on speaking terms when I left to go home for the funeral. I was really surprised."

"Wow, congratulations, love. We have a wedding to plan!" Brooke said, screaming into the phone.

Reign's excitement was not as obvious as Brooke's but I knew she was happy for me. We continued the conversation a little while longer. I promised to send them the video once I received a copy from Remington. We all agreed to meet up over the weekend to celebrate and talk about next steps.

I continued to make breakfast while Remington continued to work upstairs. Once I was done I called for him to come down and eat while the food was hot. Remington made his way downstairs. The first few minutes were silent.

"What kind of wedding do you want?" Remington asked.

"Umm, nothing too big. What about you?"

"Doesn't matter to me. I just want to marry you and make sure the girls are there. All else doesn't matter."

"Awe, that's sweet Remington."

I got off the barstool and made my way to him. I kissed him on the lips and was ready to get back to my food. Remington was not having it. He gently pushed the back of my neck and deepened the kiss. At that moment, I knew breakfast was no longer a priority for either of us.

"Let's go into the conversation room."

Remington didn't utter a word but the smirk on his face said it all. We spent the next twenty minutes in the conversation room making love in the random places we saw fit. If this was what the engagement and married life would be like, I'm definitely looking forward to what this new level brings for us.

After our love making session, Remington and I decided to try eating breakfast again. This time we ate in silence. Honestly, my mind was all over the place and I was happy for the silence. For the first time, my mind racing was a good thing. I was thinking about wedding plans, transition plans, etc. I was excited but exhausted from thinking of everything that needed to be planned. Thank goodness I had Brooke and Reign.

Remington and I decided to plan an engagement party. He wanted to start the process of buying a house before the wedding and I was fine with that. The last thing I wanted to do was start off the marriage moving and doing a lot of unnecessary work. I decided to put my efforts into planning the engagement party and let him focus on finding the right house.

I gave him a list of my must-haves and I left the rest up to him.

Remington and I spent the rest of the day together doing nothing. I was thankful for the break. My brain was working overtime with all the things that needed to happen. Plan the engagement party. Find a house. Plan the wedding. My absolute favorite part was to figure what countries we were going to visit on our two week honeymoon. I couldn't believe he had actually agreed to going out of the country with me for two weeks. Remington Slayton not working for two weeks. Well, I knew he would work but at least not being in the office for two weeks. I would have him all to myself most days and I could hardly wait. Of course, I had taken the liberty of planning our honeymoon as well. I was excited but mentally exhausted.

I laid in Remington's lap as he watched one of his many favorite television shows, The Black List. I was enjoying the peace and quiet until Remington's phone began to buzz like crazy.

"Will you please answer your phone?"

"It's not important. It can wait until tomorrow."

"It must be important if they are calling back to back."

"Alexis, it's not important. I'll answer if I feel it's important."

"Damn, you don't have to get all pissy. It's actually annoying for it to just be buzzing constantly like that."

"Fine, I'll turn the damn phone off."

"Don't do it on my account. I'll just go get in my bed. Damn."

"Come on baby, let's not let something as petty as a buzzing phone ruin our vibe."

"You're right. Just turn it off because it is annoying."

Remington turned his phone off and continued to enjoy his show. I relaxed back into his lap and closed my eyes.

The Lies

It was hard to believe that it had been three months since Remington's proposal. So much had happened. Here I was, standing in the middle of our new house panicking about the million and one things that still needed to be done before guests arrived for our engagement party. What was supposed to be a small, intimate gathering turned into this grandiose event. We were now expecting more than seventy-five guests. We had more than enough inside and outside space to accommodate the guests. It's just that there were so many people and the introvert in me was screaming. I needed like fifteen minutes to myself. I asked my mom and sister to direct the setup of the backyard while I took a break. If anyone understood my need for a break, it was them.

"Will you two make sure they set up the tents and chairs the way it should be? I need fifteen minutes to myself."

"Are you okay, baby?" Mom asked.

"Yes, I just need a few minutes to get myself together before it gets crazy around here. Plus, I'm going to call Remington to check on him. He should've been back hours ago."

"Okay, we'll make sure everything is in order."

I exited the room and headed to the master suite. It really hadn't dawned on me how long Remington had been gone until I mentioned it to my mom. I pulled my phone from my back pocket and called him. His phone went straight to voicemail. Maybe he didn't charge it. That's typical Remington behavior. I decided to call his business line. It rang twice and then it was sent to voicemail. So, I left a voicemail: *Hi, Remington. It's me. I'm checking to see where you are and to make sure you are okay. Give me a call when you get this message. I love you, bye.*

I sat in the accent chair in our bedroom and stared into space. I hope Remington and the girls are okay. If I don't hear from him soon, I'm going to call the girls' mom to see what time they left. I decided to text his sisters in the group chat we started shortly after Remington and I announced our engagement.

Alexis: Hey Synthia and Santoria! When are y'all getting to the house? And have either of you spoken with your brother? He hasn't made it back from picking up the girls yet.

A few minutes passed and I finally got a response from Santoria.

Santoria: Hey Lexie. I'll be over in the next couple of hours. Remington brought the girls to our hotel maybe two and a half hours ago. He said he needed to run some errands and would come pick them up when he was headed home.

Alexis: Oh really? I just tried calling him and didn't get an answer. I hope he gets them back here in time to get ready for tonight.

Synthia: If he doesn't, no worries. We will make sure they are ready. No stress for you. You need to make sure you are ready to have a damn ball.

Santoria: Sis, you must be getting them dressed because I have a hard time getting myself and my crew ready. I'm not adding two high maintenance girls to the list.

Synthia: They have a grandma for a reason. Mom will make sure they are dressed and ready to go if need be.

Alexis: LOL! Thanks y'all. I wish Remington would answer his damn phone.

Synthia: His ugly self needs to because I have called a couple of times, too.

Santoria: I hope he's not getting cold feet. It's just the damn engagement.

Synthia: That is not funny San. Alexis, she is just joking.

Alexis: If he is, it's money he spent. Not me.

That was the end of our text conversation but I really meant what I said. It had been a while since Remington pulled one of his disappearing acts. I just found it strange that he pulled this mess anytime something important was happening. I was not about to let it mess up my mood. I sat in silence for a few more minutes before joining my mom and my sister back in the family room.

I found them looking out the floor to ceiling windows that provided the best view of the backyard. I was blown away at how nice the set up looked so far. There were twelve tents set up. One would be for food, one for drinks and dessert, and the other ten would be for guests. The food and drink tents were the only ones not connected. The other ten were connected some type of way. I was so excited to see the finished product.

"It's looking really good, Lexis," my sister, Monica, said.

"Yeah, it is huh? I can't wait to see it with the lights and the tables decorated as well."

"Did you get Remington on the phone?" Mom asked.

"No, he didn't answer but he's made it back from picking up the girls. They are with his sister."

"Oh okay. I hope he's okay."

"I'm sure he is. He told his sister he needed to run some errands."

Mom was silent after that and it seemed like her mood changed quickly. I didn't have time to dwell on it. My thoughts were interrupted by the sound of Brooke, Reign, and Justice's voices. Yes, the backup had finally arrived. I know I had gotten on my mom and my sister's nerves. My brother and his family were still at the hotel as was my dad and his new wife. I still wasn't sure if I was a fan of hers yet. Mom didn't seem to mind her so I guess I shouldn't either.

With the help of my crew, I was able to get the ball rolling on a lot of things. I delegated a lot of tasks to my mom, Monica, Brooke, Reign, Justice, Synthia, and Santoria. As promised, they made it to the house a couple hours after our texting. They didn't have the kids with them. They left them back at the hotel with their spouses and parents. Remington still hadn't shown up or answered his phone. I was worried but I didn't call him again. Both Synthia and Santoria tried calling but he didn't answer for them either.

I was in the master suite getting my makeup done when I heard Remington's voice. It was an hour and a half before the party was expected to start and he was just making it back home. I was pissed but I was going to play it cool since we had a house full of guests. He entered our bedroom in pure Remington style. Loud and attempting to crack a joke. I asked the makeup artist to give us a few minutes.

"Remington, I have been calling you all day. Where have you been?""

"I had to finish up something really quick and my phone died."

"You didn't think I needed to know you and the girls made it back safely?"

"I didn't want to bother you when I knew you would be over here getting things ready for tonight, baby."

"It would've been nice to have your assistance for OUR engagement party. Instead, you decide today is the perfect day to go get work done for hours."

"I didn't think it was that big of a deal. You have plenty of help here."

"Whatever."

I decided it wasn't worth going back and forth with him. I stepped outside the room and asked the makeup artist to come back inside to finish my face so I could get dressed. Remington decided he would shower and get dressed in the bathroom in the basement. I was so pissed that I could hardly function.

However, my mood changed when I put on my dress. I chose a rose gold, strapless, sequin dress. It fit like a glove. The v-cut that showed off my girls was amazing but not as amazing as the train on the dress. I wore the black diamond teardrop earrings and black diamond teardrop necklace that Remington surprised me with a few weeks ago. I also wore the black shoes that I wore the night he proposed. I was rocking my natural hair and my makeup was more on the dramatic side. I went for a dramatic smokey eye. I felt amazing and looked amazing. Finally, I was dressed. I sprayed my favorite perfume, Michael Kors Wanderlust, grabbed my clutch and headed out of our bedroom.

My phone was in my clutch and I felt it buzz. I pulled out the phone and saw I had a text from Nikki.

Nikki: Congratulations on your engagement. I hope Remington is worth the trouble.

"Umm, odd," I said out loud.

"What's odd?" Brooke asked.

"This text I just received from Nicole, Nikki or whatever she wants to be called."

"What did it say?" I showed Brooke the message and she frowned her face up. "That is weird. Did they use to mess around or something? She sounds bitter and jealous."

"I don't think so. I don't even know how to respond to this message."

"You don't. It's your engagement party. We have no time for bad vibes."

"You're right."

"By the way, you look fucking fabulous! Stunning. This dress is banging."

"I love this dress and I feel fucking fabulous."

I made my way into the living room and headed to the backyard where my parents and Remington's parents were.

Guests hadn't started to arrive yet but I knew it was only a matter of time before they did. I pulled my phone out to text my brother to see where the hell he was. Just as I finished my text, Reign walked by and snatched my phone.

"You won't be needing this tonight. You can trust me with it for the night."

"Girl, if you don't give me my phone we are going to have problems."

"You need to enjoy your night and this phone will prohibit that. Damn just for one night, Lexie."

"Sure. Keep it but you are responsible for giving people directions when they need it."

"I can do that. Now, let's take a look at how great everything looks inside and out. Remington outdid himself."

I rolled my eyes at the mention of his name. Obviously, Reign didn't see it or didn't care to ask what my problem was. We walked through the kitchen and dining room. There had to be at least ten dozen black roses in the two rooms. We made our way to the backyard and it was gorgeous. I requested centerpieces with black and rose gold. I was surprised to find random pictures of Remington and myself on all the tables. What I didn't notice at first is each picture had a quote with it. It was the sweetest gesture. I could hardly hold back the tears. I loved Remington, even with his flaws. He could piss me off but I was always reminded of how sweet and thoughtful he was.

I reached in my clutch to get my phone to text him but I remembered the Reign had taken my phone.

"Where is Remington?"

"I think he's still getting dressed," Mrs. Slayton responded.

"Oh okay." I hadn't realized that she was standing that close to me.

"He loves you, Alexis. I hope you know that and will always remember that."

"Yes, I know he does."

His mom didn't say anything else before she walked away. Both Reign and I looked at each other like what the fuck was that about. Anyway, I wanted to go love on my man before we were inundated with guests.

"I'm going to go inside and find Remington before all the guests arrive."

"Okay, just don't try to get your fifteen minute freak on and mess up your makeup."

"Shut up."

I went straight to the basement where Remington was getting dressed. I could hear him on the phone. He sounded frustrated but I couldn't really make out his words. When I walked into the room he immediately ended the conversation. It was like he hung up on the person.

"Is everything okay?"

"Yes, work shit. The usual. You look amazing as usual."

I could tell he was deflecting. Remington was the king of deflection.

"Thanks. And thanks for the sweet notes and the pictures and for everything really."

"Of course. Anything for you, the future Mrs. Slayton."

I made the mistake of brushing my lips against Remington's for a light kiss. He pulled me by the waist and demanded more. As he deepened the kiss, I moaned and became aroused. I knew at that very moment I needed to have Remington. I needed to feel him inside of me and savor the taste of his skin on my tongue. And it was so. We both had our fix of each other. It wasn't the wild, untamed sex that we were accustomed to but it was the fix we needed. I left the basement feeling twenty pounds lighter.

By the time Remington and I got upstairs, more guests had arrived and the party was really getting started. The DJ had set up his equipment and began playing music. The kids were set up in the family room with all their amenities to keep them busy and out of the way of the adults.

Remington grabbed my hand and we entered the back yard hand in hand. We were met by a standing ovation. I glanced at Remington and he winked.

"Ladies and Gentlemen, the future Mr. and Mrs. Remington Slayton," the DJ announced. Nothing sounded better than that announcement. If nothing else went according to plan, I would be happy just from that simple announcement.

As guests continued to arrive, Remington and I made our rounds. Eventually, an announcement was made that it was time for dinner. Everyone gathered to fix their plates. Brooklyn advised Remington and I to remain seated as we would be served. The DJ played all the R&B hits from the late 90s and early 2000s. Blackstreet, *Before I Let You Go,* was playing and I was jamming. Remington leaned in closely and brushed his tongue across my earlobe.

"Baby, where is your phone?"

"Reign took it from me. She didn't want me to be distracted by it tonight. Why?"

"I was just wondering."

I noticed Remington had a slight grimace on his face. I also noticed that he had checked his phone several times since we had been seated.

"Is everything okay, Remington? You seem distracted."

"Yes, it's fine. I was trying to respond to a few texts and emails but it can wait."

"That would be great. If I'm without my phone you need to be without yours tonight."

"You're right."

He put his phone in his pocket and we continued to enjoy the music. It wasn't long before Brooklyn and Justice brought our plates. In true Remington style, he had to make an announcement. He tapped his wine glass and everyone turned in our direction.

"I'd like to say something. Many of you know me as a jokester. For once, I'd like to be serious. At least for the moment." He then turned to me and began to speak. "Alexis, I've never felt so blessed. You are everything I need or want in a woman. I couldn't think of anyone else I would want to call my partner in life, partner in crime, or Mrs. Slayton. I've been on cloud nine since you agreed to be my wife. So, here's to our future. May we always remember why we chose love."

I sat quietly with tears in my eyes. My emotional moment was stolen when Reign started chanting, "speech, speech, speech." All I could think was this heifer knows I don't like speaking in front of crowds. I felt obligated to respond to Remington's sweet message though.

Standing, I turned towards Remington and said what I felt in that moment.

"Remington, thank you for choosing me. You're lucky to have me." I winked and continued speaking. "Seriously, you are my safe place. Your love exceeds anything I have experienced. I admire your ambition but most importantly, I admire your ability to be a great father, businessman, and now fiancé. While we will use this engagement period to work on our relationship, I'm confident this union is divine. I love you and I will continue to love you. You are the sun to my shine. You are the rain to my bow. You are my everything. I love you, baby! And I can't wait to be Mrs. Slayton."

Just as I was finishing up my lil spiel, the DJ played *Heard About Us* from The Carters album. It was the perfect song. It was actually one of my favorite songs. Remington and I embraced each other and of course he did the most. The kiss he bestowed upon me was a bit much to be in the presence of company. Remington didn't care. I guess I shouldn't have either but it was weird having seventy-five plus people watching me kiss so passionately.

We finally took our seats to enjoy the delicious meal. My plate consisted of honey glazed salmon, smoked gouda mac and cheese, grilled brussel sprouts, and a dinner roll. Remington's plate consisted of grilled steak, smoked gouda mac and cheese, steamed green beans, and a dinner roll. I enjoyed my meal and a nice crisp glass of chardonnay. Remington opted out of wine and enjoyed a nice glass of rum punch and had a shot of Don Julio waiting for him. It seemed like a bit much.

As we sat and enjoyed dinner, several guests made their way to our table to congratulate us. Honestly, the introvert in me needed a few minutes alone. Shortly after I finished dinner, I excused myself and headed to the restroom. Monica and Reign decided to join me. Great, all I wanted was some time to myself and here come these two.

"Sissy, you need a break already?"

"Girl, you know your sister. Yes, I need like ten minutes to myself. It's been a lot of smiling and talking going on," I said.

"You need to get used to this life. Remington seems to enjoy it and if I had to guess this is the life he wants to live," Reign chimed in.

"It appears he is in his element but I'm not so I hope we can find a compromise."

As we were headed to the master bedroom, the doorbell rang.

"I wonder who that is because I'm sure everyone on the guest list has already made it."

"Don't worry. I'll get the door and see who it is. You and Reign head on back. I'll be there shortly."

Reign and I continued down the hall while my sister turned back to answer the door. Reign and I spent maybe twenty minutes away from the crowd but my sister never made it to the bedroom with us. Finally, we emerged from the bedroom. When we exited to the backyard the vibe had changed significantly. It seemed everyone had weird looks on their faces. I searched the crowd for Remington but he was nowhere to be found.

I walked over to where Synthia and Santoria were. "Where's Remington?"

"He had an emergency and had to leave," Synthia responded, quickly.

"An emergency? What kind of emergency? Why didn't anyone come get me or call me?"

"He said we didn't need to and that he would call you shortly."

I didn't say anything. I just turned and walked away. My gut told me that something was not right. As I was heading towards Reign to get my phone back, my sister pulled me to the side.

"Who is Nikki or Nicole?"

"Umm, she used to work with Remington. Actually, I worked with her for a little while on my book project. Why?"

"That's who was at the door. She came here to cause a scene. She actually acted a pure ass, demanding to speak with you or Remington."

"What? Why? What did she say or do?"

"Just a bunch of loud talking, cursing, etc."

"Why didn't you come get me?"

"You know damn well I was not letting that skank close to you. If she wasn't pregnant, I would've popped her lil' ass in the damn mouth."

"Wait, what? She's pregnant?"

"Yes, like seven or eight months pregnant."

My stomach started doing flips and I became nauseous. I needed to get my phone from Reign and find out where the hell Remington was and why Nikki showed up at our house acting a damn fool.

I walked away from my sister and made my way to Reign, Brooklyn, and Justice. They all had looks on their faces that did not make me feel any better.

"Reign, I need my phone so I can call Remington."

"Okay, but let's go inside first."

"Why? I just need my phone."

"Lexie, I'm not sure what's going on but I know you won't be happy when you get your phone so I would rather we go inside in a more secluded area away from guests."

"What the hell is going?" I knew I had raised my voice slightly but I was getting so damn frustrated. I just wanted my fucking phone. However, I obliged, walked inside, and headed towards the kitchen. I had four people on my heels. My sister, Reign, Brooklyn, and Justice. Geesh, I needed a few fucking minutes to myself.

When I finally got my phone I looked at my call log and saw I had thirty-four missed calls from Nikki. Instinctively, I checked my text messages as well. I had well over fifty messages from her. I'm not sure why but I didn't bother reading them right away. My phone dinged and I saw I had a message from Remington.

Remington: Reign, do not give Lexie this phone back.

Oh, he thought Reign still had my phone.

Alexis: I have my phone already and I need to know 1) where are you and 2) what the hell is going on.

I didn't get an immediate response from Remington so I decided to start going through the messages from Nicole.

Nikki: Marrying Remington would be a horrible mistake for you.

Nikki: Has he even told you about us?

Nikki: I'm sure he hasn't. He always fails to mention the family we are building over here.

She attached a picture of a sonogram. My heart dropped. I should've stopped reading but I continued and it was like my life with Remington was a big ass lie.

Nikki: Yes, I'm pregnant with a boy. And yes, it's Remington's child.

Nikki: He claimed he told you and y'all were working through it.

Nikki: To his credit, he did try to get me to get an abortion. He even drove me to Charlotte the night that your uncle passed.

Nikki: Of course, I wasn't having any of that. I don't care what the circumstances are. I'm not aborting our child.

Nikki: Remington is trash. What type of man does not take full responsibility for his family?

Nikki: I just don't want you to make the mistake of marrying him.

Nikki: That's why I showed up at the house tonight. But you know Remington, he tried to handle it.

Nikki: He's here now begging me to not tell you the truth. He's a sad case.

Nikki: All he does is lie. He's manipulative and deceitful.

I stopped reading. Everything seemed like such a blur. I could not believe this was happening right now at this very moment. This was supposed to be one of the best days of our lives. This whole fairytale of Remington and I has been built on a lie. My chest began to pound. I was brought out of my trance by the faint sound of voices. My mom, Monica, Reign, Brooklyn, and Justice were all around me talking. I hadn't even realized they were speaking to me. I put my phone down.

"Okay, y'all. I will be fine. First things first, I'm going to pack some clothes and leave. I need to get away."

"Come home with me tomorrow, baby."

"No, Mom. I don't want to be in Tennessee. I think I'm going to fall off the grid for a while but I will let all of you know where I am and I will check in periodically. I really need to wrap my mind around this." Before I knew it, I was sobbing.

This is not what I envisioned. I trusted him with my life. He has another woman pregnant. A fucking woman that I've worked closely with. I just want to pack my bags and leave this lie of a life we have built.

"Let's get you packed and quickly," Monica said.

"Right. Let's get this done quickly," Reign chimed in.

"Wait, where is his family right now?" I asked.

"They left a few minutes ago," Monica said.

I headed down the hall to my bedroom and started to pull things out of the closet. I had no idea where I was going or what I should pack. I just wanted to get the hell away from this house and Remington. I sold my damn house for this shit. I didn't realize I said it out loud until my mom asked if I said something.

"Nothing, Mom."

We packed about three weeks worth of clothes and I changed into more comfortable clothes as well. I made sure I had all my electronic devices and charges. I went into the kitchen, left my engagement ring on the island, and headed to my car.

"Brooke, can Mom and I stay at your house tonight?"

"Of course, that's not a question. Monica, do you want to stay as well?"

"No, I'll get a room at the same hotel as our brother."

"Okay, we're headed to Brooke's if you want to come by there first," I said.

"We will all be over," Justice responded.

Mom and I put our luggage in my car and we left the house. As soon as we started enroute to Brooke's house, my phone rang and it was Remington. I didn't bother answering. I hit ignore. He called continuously and I ignored each one. The nerve of him. I wish all this was a damn nightmare. Sadly, it was my life at the moment.

After twenty minutes of driving, we arrived at Brooke's house. I parked my car in the garage beside hers. Justice, Reign, and Monica all parked in the driveway. There was a reason I chose Brooke's house and not Reign's. Remington didn't know where Brooke lived but he knew the area in which Reign lived. Not the exact address, but he had some idea. I just wanted to avoid him because I wasn't ready to talk. Hell, my mind was still reeling with all the messages from Nikki. Messages I had yet to get all the way through. Emotionally, I was exhausted but my body was so restless.

"Do you need anything?"

"No, Mom. I'm fine. I'll get a glass of wine and start figuring out what's next."

"Don't rush it, baby. Take your time. Rome wasn't built in a day. Rebuilding after Remington won't happen overnight."

"I know. I just feel so stupid. Like how did I miss all of this?"

"Love. We can sometimes be blinded by love."

"I sold my house so we could get ours. I have nowhere to live."

"You always have a place to live. It's up to you to move back."

"I love the life I've built here in Atlanta and I just don't want to leave that behind."

"And you won't. Stay here. You have a support system here and afar. Remember that. Now, go get that glass of wine."

"I love you, Mom."

"I love you, too, Alexis. Always."

We exited the car to find the others in the house opening bottles of wine. I grabbed a glass and poured Pinot. The cold, crisp taste hit my tongue and I was relieved that something still seemed normal in my life. I knew everyone was waiting for me to address the elephant in the room.

"I think I'm going to Lake Tahoe for a week or so. Afterwards, I will go to Lake Travis outside of Austin. Then I will come home and relax. When I get back to Georgia, I will figure out my next move. So, Brooke and Reign, I'll need somewhere to lay my head while I figure it out."

"Why don't you come to Maryland with me for a while?" Monica asked.

"I may do that, too."

The room fell silent but it was short lived as my phone began ringing again. I looked down to see it was Nikki calling. What else could she want?

"Don't answer it, Lexie. Just let it ring. She's done enough talking for the night."

I didn't respond to Justice. I was so tempted to answer and ask her what more she had to say but for my peace of mind I ignored the phone call. Less than two minutes later, Remington was calling my phone repeatedly. Finally, I made the smart decision of turning my phone off.

I grabbed my laptop and purse out of my car and headed back in to start booking flights and AirBnBs for the next two weeks. The only flight that wasn't hella expensive was my flight to Tennessee. Making travel arrangements was a relief. At least, I knew what the next three weeks of my life would be like. I just needed to reschedule in-person client meetings to virtual meetings.

"My flight to Lake Tahoe leaves at 10:30 in the morning. Who can take me to the airport?"

"I can," Brooke, Reign, and Justice answered.

"I'll take her. She's staying here. It makes no sense for either of you to drive over here to get her to the airport."

"Thanks, Brooke. Just don't have me late." We all laughed. Brooke was notorious for being late. It felt good to laugh, even for just a moment.

We all made small talk before Mom decided she was headed upstairs to shower and get in the bed. Monica decided it was time to head to the hotel. Apparently, she made her reservation on the car drive over to Brooke's house. I hugged them both and said good night. Brooke, Reign, Justice and I moved to the living room to be more comfortable.

"Whew, this has been a long, crazy day," I said.

"It has been a lot. How are you feeling?" Reign asked.

"Like my whole fucking world just fell apart."

"That's an accurate feeling. Remington has a lot of explaining to do," Justice responded.

"Honestly, I don't want to hear shit he has to say. He has a whole baby on the way. He was really building a whole life with Nikki and I had no idea. Talk about feeling stupid." I couldn't suppress the tears that escaped and rolled down my cheeks. I had never felt so defeated before in my life.

"He hid it well, Lexie. Don't beat yourself up over his bullshit," Reign said.

"Yeah, this shit is on him and has more to do with him as a person than you as a girlfriend. He has issues," Brooke chimed in.

"I know but it just hurts like hell. I thought we were building something special. I thought he was my person. I feel stupid parading around with that damn ring on my finger, selling my house, buying a house with him and he has all this going on right under my nose."

"You didn't know. You fell in love with the person he wanted you to fall in love with. You fell in love with his representative and not who he is," Reign all but screamed.

"I'm just happy you found out before you married him," Justice whispered.

"Yeah, me too. I'm going to reach out to a real estate attorney on Monday. I need to find out how to get my name off the house."

"You don't want to keep it?" Brooke asked.

"No, I don't want that much house. I'll find something more suitable for a single person."

"When do you plan to get all your things out?" Justice asked.

"I'll hire movers and have them pack it up and put it in storage until I figure out where I'll be living. I may just find a house to rent for a year so I won't have to wait on the closing process. Shit, who knows?"

"Take your time. No need to rush. You have us and you can always crash at my or Brooke's house for a while," Reign said.

"Yeah, but I'll want my own space. You all know how I am sometimes." We all laughed because I could be the biggest introvert at times. When I needed time to myself I needed to be in my own space. "Thank y'all for being so supportive. I love y'all for it."

"Girl, hush. We got you always," Reign said.

"Alway!" Brooke chimed in.

Justice looked over at me and mouthed, *"Always."*

I smiled. There was no way I was ready to leave this crew and the life I built in Atlanta because of Remington's raggedy ass. Just the thought of him made me sad. He is such a fraud. I don't even know who he is. Suddenly, I felt physically exhausted and I wanted nothing more than to go to sleep.

"I'm going to bed. I need some rest."

I hugged Brooke, Reign, and Justice and headed upstairs. I felt the strongest urge to cry. I'm not even sure how to move forward from this point. Going away seemed like the most logical thing to do. Travel was a good stress reliever for me and honestly I didn't want to intrude on Brooke and Reign. And there was no way I was going back to the house with Remington. My heart broke at the very thought of him. I needed time to wrap my mind around the events of the day.

I washed my face and climbed into bed. As soon as my head hit the pillow, I felt like I was being suffocated with questions. Why did he pretend so well? Why didn't I see this coming? What did I overlook? What was I going to do now? It was all overwhelming so I cried myself to sleep. I'm not sure when I fell asleep but I was awakened by a nightmare or what was now my reality. In the dream, I stood in the grand entry at our house and watched a very pregnant Nikki roll her luggage in and head down the hall to the master bedroom. Shocked, I followed her and noticed one of the guest bedrooms had been turned into a nursery for the baby.

I woke up out of my sleep whimpering. I wanted this part of my life to be over. I wanted to go back to what I thought it was a few hours ago. I wanted to still be happily in love with Remington and enjoying our engagement party. It was all ruined. I grabbed my phone to check the time only to realize I never turned it on from earlier. I waited impatiently as it powered on. I had so many notifications as I figured I would. I had over fifty missed calls from Remington. Of course, there were text messages from both him and Nikki. Both his sisters had texted as well. I also noticed I had so many email notifications. Curiosity got the best of me and I started going through the emails.

Nikki had forwarded several emails between her and Remington. The first email was from their trip to New York. Funny, I remember that weekend because we had plans but they were changed last minute because of a business opportunity. Remington was in New York for five days that time.

I didn't see the original email she sent to him but I read his response.

Remington Slayton

To: Nicole

Damn…I'm just now getting a chance to really read your email…Okay yes, I agree with you…this back and forth shit is getting old. But what I'm starting to believe is you sabotaged us getting closer on purpose… I haven't really figured out why though… Besides your family who cares about you, I'm probably the only male that is not just trying to fuck you but really fuck with you and have a genuine care for you and want to see you grow to be great! I don't really see where the "dishonesty" statements come from. I've never done anything to hurt you, I've always treated you with respect despite our little bouts… I've always encouraged you to move on your ideas and aspirations. Never asked you for anything nor have I ever tried to use you for anything. You not thinking I was coming to New York is a tell tell sign, too… I've always done whatever I've told you I would do and if things did change I always let you know. I really made it my business to get to New York. I even paid babysitters to help my little sister out while I was gone. I know you may not believe it but I did have a little quick day planned for us before we left, receipts and tickets to prove it, but that doesn't matter now. The fact that you thought I left you did bother me a little bit and you wouldn't even *listen to the reason…What I know about you is you sleep late… what I know about me is I rise early…I figured me and Tonio would take care of a little business, get a few videos and pictures then come back through to get you or send you a meet up address when it was check out time. Chinatown was literally 15 minutes away…then you try to downplay me as a man because of what was obviously misunderstood or miscommunicated. Which further makes me want to believe you sabotaged us on purpose. I really enjoyed myself with you. From the ripping and running to meet up with you at the airport to how curious you seemed about the presentation. To how relaxed and happy you acted at Tonic the first night. Obviously, I was way off and what happened the last day threw me for a big loop. I'll wrap it up with this though, for our second time being out of town together (Charleston was 1st) I think it was great. I enjoyed your company…I like seeing you smile…I'll put your key in the mail tomorrow… Let me know when you're ready to start packing and moving. I'll help get it done no problem!*

I sat in disbelief after reading the emails between Remington and Nikki. He was such a fraud. All this time, he was chasing her and going out of town with her but telling me she was crazy. No wonder he didn't want me working with her anymore. It was too close for comfort to his big ass lie getting out. He had some real issues. He tried to play on her insecurities in that email and he's found a way to manipulate me as well.

I didn't bother reading any of the text messages I received from Remington, his sisters, or Nikki. I saw my brother had text asking if I was okay. I sent him a quick text back.

Alexis: No, I'm not but I will be. Sorry this whole ordeal was a waste of your time.

I couldn't get back to sleep. I tossed and turned all night. I laid in bed looking at the ceiling when my phone rang. I didn't have to look at the caller ID to know who it was. Against my better judgement, I answered the phone.

"What?"

"Alexis, please come home so we can talk."

"Home? This whole fake ass relationship has been built on lies."

"I can explain. Just give me a chance."

"You can't explain shit. You didn't bother telling me you had a whole fucking baby on the way."

"I don't know if it's really my baby."

"The fact that's even a possibility is the fucking problem. And you might want to check Nikki because she's on a roll with exposing you."

"What do you mean?"

"Screen shot all your text conversations, forwarded all the emails, etc. Oh yeah, how was your trip to New York?"

"She told you about that?"

"Nah, she just forwarded me the email and all the text messages."

"Lexie, I can explain."

"Can you really? Because you are not doing much of it."

"I want to talk to you face to face."

"We have nothing that can't be discussed via phone."

"Come home. Let's talk and work on us. And put your damn ring back on."

"You have lost your fucking mind. That ring doesn't mean a damn thing. It was all a lie."

"Don't say that because you know that's not true."

"Remington, you have another woman pregnant. She came to our house tonight during our engagement party and you left with her. I think I know where your priorities are."

"I was trying to avoid causing a scene when we should have been celebrating."

"You should've been trying to tell me the fucking truth before you brought me into this mess. Got me out here parading through the city with a fucking engagement ring on while you are out here building a whole family with someone else."

"I'm not building a family with Nicole. It was a slip up and she had a change of heart about the abortion."

"First off, it wasn't a slip up. Y'all out spending quality time, taking trips, going on dates. It was a whole fucking relationship."

"Alexis Carter, I was not and am not in a relationship with Nicole."

"Remington Slayton, you are a liar, a cheat, and a master manipulator. And I hate that I sold my house to move in with your lying ass."

"Lexie, that was harsh. Watch how you talk to me."

"Fuck you. I shouldn't be talking to you period. Matter of fact, Don't contact me again. I'll call you when I'm ready to get my shit out of that house. "

"You won't get a damn thing out of my house."

"Your house? Boy you have lost all your damn mind."

"I'm changing the locks."

"Fine, I'll show up with the cops and still get my shit. Better yet, I'll have my attorney contact you or your attorney if you get one."

I hung up the phone before he could say anything else. The nerve of his punk ass to even think he could tell me how to talk to him. I tossed and turned the rest of the morning. I finally dragged myself out of bed and to the shower around six o'clock. I wasn't surprised that Mom was up.

"Good morning, Mommy."

"Hey baby. You okay this morning?"

"No, but I will be as soon as I get on this plane and sort through my thoughts."

"Running away won't fix the problem but take the time you need to regroup."

"I know. I'm not running away, Momma. I just need some time to myself for a few days."

"Okay, I'm always here if you want to talk. Always remember, you are the upgrade. There are no upgrades after you."

I laughed. I needed that chuckle early this morning. Leave it to my mom to remind me I'm the true catch. Mommas always know what to say.

My body was so tense and no matter how much I tried to escape the heaviness of what was happening, I couldn't. I leaned against the shower wall and replayed the conversation over and over in my head. I also replayed all the emails I received from Nikki. I just couldn't help thinking how naïve I had been about this whole situation. Remington and Nikki were messing around way before I came into the picture. While Remington tried to downplay their relationship, I think they really care about each other. That reality hurt more than I expected. The tears began to roll down my cheeks. The sting from my tears lingered longer than I wanted. This is so fucking crazy. My own voice startled me. I didn't realize I was speaking out loud.

I stayed in the shower longer than usual. I wanted to relax and hot water usually did the trick and I tried keeping a steaming hot towel on my eyes to alleviate the swelling. I was unsuccessful with both. I looked in the mirror and realized I looked like shit but I think I looked better than I felt. I dressed quickly and headed downstairs.

I found Mom and Brooke in the kitchen eating breakfast. I rolled my eyes slightly. Of course, Mom made breakfast. We had fresh homemade biscuits, salmon croquettes, and house potatoes. It smelled delicious and looked even better. I tried to force myself to eat but my appetite was nonexistent. It was finally time for me to head to the airport and I was happy about it.

Brooke got me to the airport in record time. I hugged Brooke and Mom before disappearing into the Hartsfield Jackson International Airport. I headed to the Delta kiosk to check in for my flight. Check-in was smooth and getting through the security checkpoint was even easier with TSA pre-check. I made it to my gate with plenty of time to spare. I was tempted to go through all the text messages I had from Nikki, Remington, Remington's sisters, and everyone else texting to check on me but quickly decided against it. Just as I was about to put my phone up, it dinged. I looked to see it was a new message from Nikki. Damn, she's relentless. I clicked the message and began to read the last message.

Nikki: I will not reach out after this last message. But what type of man would want the woman he loves to know and work with the other woman? He's petty and careless. He hasn't thought about your feelings not one time. He's calling me to tell me what you are saying. WTH!! He hasn't considered either of us in this situation. But honestly I think you are a good woman and wish you the best.

Alexis: Nikki I have no ill feelings to you or for you. None. I've never been in a situation like this. I don't do drama. I don't degrade other women. I'm not that type of woman. I wasn't raised like that. I have nothing to hide or no shame. So, I'm not sure what he's telling you. Things are what they are. I appreciate you reaching out and shedding light on this fucked up situation. I've done what I've been taught to do. Own the situation. It's fucked up. I got played by a guy I thought was my person. He obviously played his role well. I wish you two the best raising your child. Best wishes!

I really hoped that was the last time she would reach out to me. As luck would have it, my phone began ringing and it was Remington. I was not in the mood to speak with him. I declined the call and put my phone on vibrate. Thank goodness for my kindle. I was going to get lost in someone else's fantasy being that mine had fallen apart so quickly. I selected a Brenda Jackson book from the Westmoreland series. My phone vibrated. I looked down to see a text from Remington.

Remington: Alexis, please cease all contact with Nikki. I'm asking you to do this for me please.

The nerve of him to try and tell me who to communicate with. Before I realized it I was responding to his message.

Alexis: Remington, please note you are not in a position in my life to request anything from me. If you are concerned about communication, I suggest you have your girlfriend stop contacting me. Better yet, how about you stop contacting me.

Remington: You are being childish and unreasonable. Let's be adults about this situation.

Alexis: Fuck you. Childish is proposing to me when you know damn well you are building a family with someone else. Grow the fuck up. Man the fuck up. And don't contact me again.

He didn't respond. I'm happy he didn't because I was so damn mad. I had to take ten deep breaths to calm my nerves. I tried to focus on reading but it was a lost cause. My mind was reeling with all kinds of thoughts. I wasn't sure what game Remington and Nikki were playing but I knew I didn't want any parts of it. Finally, it was time to board my flight and I couldn't have been happier.

I had plans to sleep during the flight but once I was seated my brain went into overdrive. I took my phone out and began typing in the notes section. I didn't have a specific thing to write about. I just needed to get the words out of my head. The first thing I wrote about is how well my relationship with Remington was. I was rambling. I made a mental note to get a journal before making it to my AirBnB in Lake Tahoe. I tried my hardest to relax and not think the rest of my flight.

Upon arrival at the airport, I claimed my luggage from baggage claim and headed to the rental car counter. I picked up the car and headed on my way. I did a Google search for the closest Target. I needed to grab a few things, including a journal. An hour and a half after landing at Reno-Tahoe Airport, I checked into my AirBnB. The first thing I did was change the sheets. Shortly, afterwards I took a much needed hot shower and fixed a hot cup of English Twinning Breakfast Tea.

The house had an amazing view that overlooked the lake. It was peaceful, serene, and allowed me to feel what I was feeling. I sat quietly as I tried to wrap my mind around all that had taken place in the last seventy-two hours. My thoughts were interrupted by the ringing of my phone. I didn't have to look to know it was Remington. I declined the call and turned my ringer off. While I had my phone in my hand, I sent a quick text to Brooke, Reign, Mom, and Justice letting them know I made it safely and was relaxing. Or at least attempting to relax.

I grabbed my new journal and headed out to the wraparound porch to write. I only brought my phone for the music. The words began to flow but so did the tears. I spent hours writing and crying. I had hoped I would feel better but I didn't. I'm not sure being here at Lake Tahoe was the best decision for me. I so desperately wanted my life back. I wanted Remington to be who I thought he was. I wanted to still be in Atlanta planning my wedding. I wanted to be able to see Alivia and Reagan whenever they were in town. Oh God, I'm going to miss them. I hadn't thought about not having them around. That broke my heart even more if that was possible. I felt so lonely and desperate. I couldn't rid myself of one question: Can Remington and I work this out? I just didn't see a way of that happening. He had a baby on the way.

I wanted nothing more than for him to feel a little of the pain I felt. I wanted to say I hated him but the truth is I didn't. He was my person. Flawed, but my person. At least, I thought he was. No, I desperately wanted him to be. It hurt so badly to know that he probably wasn't. He's probably not even bothered by the fact that I'm away and he has no idea where I am. I pulled out my work laptop and attempted to occupy my mind for a few hours.

I responded to client emails and reviewed a few documents. My mind constantly wandered to Remington, Nikki, their unborn son, and the twins. They were one big, happy family and here I was desperate and lonely. I hated this feeling and I wasn't sure of how to rid myself of it.

I did my second favorite thing to do outside of writing. I changed into my running clothes and headed out for a run out by the lake. The peace and serenity of running near water has always been soothing to me. I hoped it would do the trick this time around. After plugging in my music and stretching, I started on my way. I was going way faster than I thought. By the time I reached my first mile I was winded and didn't know if I would be able to make five miles as I had initially planned. I quickly decided on a three mile run. Just as I was finishing up my run I noticed a Google Hangout call from Remington. I answered it.

"What Remington?"

"Where are you, Alexis?"

"Why? What do you want?"

"I'm concerned about you."

I paused and didn't say anything for a while. He looked like shit. He didn't look like he had been crying or anything but he did look like he was stressing which was mild in comparison to how I felt.

"Why are you concerned about me? I think you've made it pretty clear where I stand with you."

"Alexis Carter, we are engaged."

"Were engaged. You know that's over."

"Lexie, I messed up. I should've told you, especially after Nicole didn't want to get the abortion."

"Nah, you should've never fucked her. How about that?"

"Well, that too but after I made the first mistake I should've come clean. Instead I tried to play cleanup."

"That's just it, Remington. It wasn't just one mistake. Y'all were a couple. Doing couple…"

"We were never a couple. I would hang out with her because she was easy. I didn't have to put in any work."

"Hmm, I didn't peg you as the lazy type. Keep talking. I'm learning a lot about you."

"Alexis, stop it."

"No, you stop it." The tears began and I couldn't stop them. "You were supposed to be my forever, Remington. You were my person. At least I thought…"

"I am your person. I just made a mistake. Stupid mistakes, but still mistakes."

"You are not my person. You introduced me to your girlfriend and let her befriend me. I guess this was all a part of your sick game."

"It's not a game, Alexis. I got caught up with Nicole. She means nothing to me."

"Apparently, I don't mean anything to you either. How could you say she means nothing to you when she's carrying your child?"

"Look, I will take care of my boy but that girl doesn't mean shit to me. Again, she was easy. No effort and just something to do."

"Something to do? What you should've been doing was tending to your woman at home. You know the one you proposed to?"

"I know, baby. I'm sorry. I don't know how to make it up but I know we can fix it. We can do counseling or whatever you want."

"Remington that won't change the fact that she's having your baby so y'all will always have ties. I just don't think I can handle that."

"You can and I can do things on your terms to make you comfortable. I need you, Alexis. You are my mine."

"I'm not yours. You only want me when it's convenient for you."

"Alexis, please come home and let's talk."

"NO!"

"You are being ridiculous. As adults, we should be able to have a conversation and decide where we're going from here."

"There's nowhere to go, Remington. I won't be able to tolerate you and an outside child."

"Well, where are you? I'll come to you."

"No, I need time to myself. I have to process what has happened and how I plan to move forward."

"You can't make that decision without me, Alexis."

"Actually Remington, I can and I will."

I ended the Google Hangout. I flopped down in the rocking chair on the porch. I had so many thoughts running through my mind. I was in no mental or emotional mindset to make a decision right now. I just know seeing Remington with an outside kid was going to be a heartbreak on repeat. I didn't want to do that to myself. Hell, I deserved better than what he was trying to give me.

I closed my eyes and rocked until my eyelids began to feel heavy. I headed inside, took a hot shower, and laid across the bed. For the first time in forty-eight hours, sleep found me. While sleep found me, so did the nightmares. I had the same nightmare over and over. I was chasing someone and Remington was chasing me. I was pregnant and the other person was holding a baby boy. I'm sure it was Nikki but I never saw a face and I couldn't tell if it was a man or woman.

Finally, I was awakened from my nightmare by the growling of my empty stomach. I had literally gone all day without eating. Thankfully, I bought groceries when I first arrived. I went into the kitchen and made a gourmet grilled cheese with mild cheddar and smoked cheddar. I also had another cup of hot tea. It was 3:38 in the morning and it was the most relaxed I'd been in days. I pulled out my laptop and clicked on Netflix. I decided to watch a few episodes of shows I'd missed out on. Before long, the sun was coming up and my eyelids were getting heavy. This is the routine I kept for the next few days. Running was helpful. Writing seemed to make me cry even more. Cooking calmed my nerves and being alone was becoming a normal thing. I decided to only text Mom and the girls to let them know I was okay. I didn't bother calling and, surprisingly, everyone respected my need to be alone.

It had been three days since my last conversation with Remington. He text daily but I hadn't responded to any correspondence from him. Hell, I didn't even bother reading his messages. It was best if I just ignored him. It was my last day at Lake Tahoe before I headed to Lake Travis in Austin. I looked forward to a change in scenery and weather. I knew Texas would be much warmer. I hoped the warmer weather and sunshine would help get me out of this funk.

I spent my last night at Lake Tahoe reading most of the book *Relationship Goals* and I enjoyed dinner from a local restaurant on the front porch. Again, my thoughts were all over the place. I had so many things to get squared away before I could decide on my next move.

I had a late morning flight the next day. I arrived in Austin and was greeted with lots of sunshine. I instantly felt my spirits lift. The next few days felt promising and I hadn't felt that in a while. I needed the hope of something great happening. After grabbing my bags from baggage claim, I headed to the rental car counter. Lake Travis didn't seem as secluded as Lake Tahoe so I didn't bother making a grocery stop. Plus, I planned to come into the city to enjoy all that 6th Street had to offer and check out other spots. After a full day of traveling, I was exhausted but I decided to give Mom a call. She answered on the second ring.

"Hey baby, how are you?"

"Hi, Mom! I'm doing okay. Better now that I'm in Texas with lots of sunshine."

"That's good to hear. How was Lake Tahoe?"

"It was okay. It served its purpose. I hope to get out more here though."

"That'll be good. Have you spoken with your brother and sister?"

"No, not yet. Is everything okay?"

"Yeah, they're fine. I think they are worried about you."

"I'll send them a text in our group chat."

"When are you coming home?"

"I'm going to spend the next five days here and then I'll come home for a few days. Then I'll go face off with my crazy reality."

"Alexis, take your time. That situation will still be there. Your emotional wellbeing is important."

"I know, Mom. That's why I'm taking my time to get back but I still have responsibilities and I need to figure out what my next move will be."

"Right. Well, home is always an option."

"I know. I just wanted to check in with you. I love you, Mommy!"

"I love you, too, baby. Try to have a little fun in Texas."

"I will."

I ended my phone call with Mom and sent a quick group text to my brother and sister.

Alexis: Hey y'all. Just checking in. I'm okay and I'm in Texas now.

I didn't get an immediate response so I put my phone down and began my relaxing process. Again, my AirBnB had an amazing view. I could see the lake from the back porch and I knew it was where I would spend the majority of my time. I grabbed a bottle of water and my journal to head out back. I began a journal entry with all the things I had learned from this relationship with Remington. The good. The bad. The ugly. I also wrote a letter to him. I'm not sure he'll ever get but it was good to get the raw emotions out. I managed to sit through my writing session without crying and that was major progress for me. I decided on a quick nap and then I would I head into the city to try a bar.

After my nap, I got dressed. Dressing up makes me feel so much better so I decided to put on head-turning clothes. I slipped on my black leather pants, black lace top, red heels, and red fedora hat. Of course, the look was completed with my favorite lipstick, Ruby Woo. I did a natural look with my makeup and headed out the door. I didn't have any specific destination and I was fine with just going with the flow. I just knew my first stop would be for food.

I did a quick Google search on the best Mexican food in Austin and settled on going to Allandale to try Fonda San Miguel. The restaurant was wonderfully decorated with Mexican art and the ambiance was really nice. I felt a small sting as I thought about

Remington. I missed him. It seemed surreal to not be communicating with him. I never thought this would be my life. It actually seemed like some shit you watch on the Lifetime Movie Network. I reeled my thoughts of Remington in and focused on the ambiance and the food before me.

I started off with a cup of Mexican corn soup with cheese. For my entree, I ordered broiled fish in garlic butter with rice and beans. The food was delicious but I didn't overstay my welcome. I headed out fairly quickly and decided to find a nice cigar lounge to relax. I found the Habana House Cigar Lounge in the city and based on the reviews, I was in for a real treat. Before I made it to the lounge, I stopped and purchased a bottle of cognac since it was BYOB.

I was greeted by one of the workers and was immediately drawn into the atmosphere. I asked a few questions and he answered them. I wasn't a cigar connoisseur by any means but I had learned a lot from Devontae and Remington. Both enjoyed their cigars. Here I was doing things that they had introduced me to and neither one of them were in my life. I discarded the negative thoughts that were attempting to set in. I managed to grab a seat in one of the comfy chairs next to a group of guys. The waiter brought me a glass of ice and I opened my bottle and lit my cigar. I was vibing to the music and zoned out. Then I heard this baritone voice.

"Excuse me, miss?"

I hadn't even realized that my eyes were closed. I opened them to find one of the guys from the table next to me speaking.

"Yes?"

"I'm Xavier. We just noticed, well I noticed how you were zoned out."

"Hi, Xavier. I'm Alexis. Yes, I'm just chilling."

"Well, would you like some company? That is if you aren't waiting on someone."

"I'm not waiting on anyone but I'd hate to take you away from your crew."

"Oh, they won't mind."

"I'm not sure I'll be much company. I'm just here to relax and clear my head."

Before Xavier could respond, one of the other guys yelled, "Man, let the lady be. She's trying to let you down nicely."

I looked up and my breath caught in my throat. This guy was gorgeous. Ruggedly handsome. He had the whole five o'clock shadow going with a tapered haircut with small soft curls atop his head, a body that was accustomed to the gym, and a caramel brown skin tone. I couldn't gauge his height while he was sitting but his long muscular legs said he was at least six feet tall. I finally pulled my eyes away from him and took a deep breath.

Xavier got the hint and finally gave in. "Well, it was nice to meet you, Alexis. Maybe I'll run into you one day when I'm not with the crew."

"Yeah, maybe so."

I didn't bother telling him that it was not going to happen being that I lived in Atlanta and was only visiting. I attempted to get back in my vibe but the baritone voice I heard earlier was ringing in my ears. Why was his voice so damn sexy?

After an hour or so, I had reached my quota for being out. I gathered my things and stood to head out. Xavier and his crew were still at the table next to me.

"Leaving so soon?" It was the guy with the deep, sexy voice.

"Yes, I've reached my quota of crowds for the day."

"Let me walk you to your car," Xavier chimed in.

"I appreciate the offer but that's not necessary. I'll be fine."

"Man, I can't get you to agree to anything with me."

"It's not personal. Enjoy your night, fellas."

"You too." They all chimed in unison.

I put an extra pep in my step since I knew I had an audience. In particular, I knew Mr. Baritone was watching as I left. It felt good to be out but the drive back to Lake Travis was longer than expected after a few glasses of cognac. I made it back to my AirBnB and crashed.

The next few days in Austin were pretty much the same. I got dressed. I went out to a different spot. I had a few drinks and relaxed. I came back to my AirBnB and crashed. It felt great to throw caution to the wind and let me hair down in the middle of my personal life crisis. I was so sad for my time in Texas to come to an end. It was the morning of my departure. I hadn't heard from Remington and was kind of sad about it. Just as I settled into my seat on my flight to head home to Tennessee, my phone dinged. I looked and saw it was a message from Remington.

Remington: Alexis, can we please talk?

Alexis: I'll let you know when I'm back in town.

Remington: Where are you? That's the least you could do is let me know your whereabouts.

Alexis: Remington you don't have that privilege anymore. But we can talk when I'm back in town in a couple of days.

Remington: Fine. Be safe. I miss you. I love you.

I decided not to respond. A couple of hours later, I was in Tennessee waiting for Mom to pick me up from the airport. I knew while I was home I would not be relaxing. Mom always found plenty for me to do. Plus, I would spend a day or two at Dad's house. I wasn't a big fan of his wife but I could tolerate Ms. Pamela for a couple days if it meant hanging with my Pops.

Mom finally arrived to pick me up and we headed straight to her favorite lunch spot in town. It was Ms. Irene's home cooked meals. This is one of the things I missed about small town living. You could always find a good home cooked meal. My mouth watered at the thought of enjoying a homemade turkey burger, fresh cut fries, and cold glass of fresh squeezed lemonade. I would top off lunch with Ms. Irene's homemade pound cake.

Mom was unusually quiet during the drive.

"Hey, you are unusually quiet. Are you okay?"

"Yes, I'm fine baby. I'm just thinking about Ms. Jackie. She's in the hospital."

"Oh, what's wrong with her?"

"She had a stroke a few days ago."

"Oh no, I'm sorry to hear that. Goodness, how's her husband?"

"He's fine. I just don't understand why folks won't be more diligent about their health."

"I know. Well, I'm happy you are diligent about yours, Momma."

"Yeah, so many of my friends would still be here if they were."

I reached over and rubbed her hand gently. Momma had lost so many of her close friends in the past few years. I hadn't realized what kind of toll those losses took on her. I really should come home more often. I wonder if she gets lonely. I really wish she would date. I wouldn't dare broach the subject right now.

For some odd reason, Remington came to mind. Not really odd, I hadn't stopped thinking about him since the whole blow up. I missed him. I wanted us back but I know that wasn't happening. I couldn't believe he was having a baby with Nikki. My mood changed instantly and I think Mom sensed it. She reached out and gently grabbed my hand.

"It will work out for you. There's a reason all of this is happening."

I didn't bother responding because I searched high and low to figure out what was the reason my life needed to be turned upside down. I couldn't find one damn reason this needed to happen when I was so happy with my relationship. I couldn't fathom anything I had done to deserve such hurt, pain, and deceit. I rode in silence as the familiar ache returned to my chest. I wanted so badly for this feeling to go away. No amount of writing or crying could fix it.

I don't even know how to begin to reconcile with Remington. I don't think a reconciliation was even possible. He had a whole child on the way. How do I get past that? I can't. As if Remington could sense my thoughts, my phone rang and it was him. I contemplated answering because I desperately wanted to hear his voice. For so long he had been my comfort in the midst of my storms. He was my safe place. Now, he was the storm and he was destroying everything I had built.

My phone dinged and I knew it was Remington texting.

Remington: Alexis, please talk to me.

Alexis: I'm headed to grab a bite to eat with Mom. I'll call you when I get home, shortly.

Remington: Home as in Atlanta or home as in your mom's house?

Alexis: Home as in Mom's house.

Remington: How long will you be in Tennessee?

Alexis: I'm not sure, Remington. I'm in no rush to get back though.

Remington: I want you to come home so we can figure out how to put this behind us.

Alexis: That's not an easy fix, Remington.

Remington: I have a plan but you have to trust me.

Alexis: Trust? Remington, that's not at the top of my list with you.

Remington: I know but at least listen to me.

Alexis: I'll call you later.

Remington: Okay, bye.

I didn't respond. Mom and I pulled up to Ms. Irene's restaurant and I was slow to get out. I wanted to believe that Remington knew how to fix this. I just didn't see a solution to this problem and it hurt so bad to think I was going to lose him. My heart wanted him so badly but my mind was screaming, NO! I was so confused. What would he do about Nikki and the baby? What would that relationship look like? How would Nikki react if we were back together? I felt so defeated because honestly I knew there was no solution to this situation. He got another woman pregnant. I just couldn't accept that.

I enjoyed lunch with Mom. We talked about everything and I knew she was just trying to keep me distracted. As much as I wanted to be good company, I knew I wasn't. I half heartedly laughed and tried my hardest to focus on what was being said to me. I just wasn't as engaged in the conversation. I felt a little guilty but my mind was racing a thousand miles per minute. I wanted to know what Remington would propose as his solution. We finished lunch and headed home. I got settled in my childhood room and told Mom I was going to take a nap. She was heading out to run a few errands.

My bedroom door had barely shut and I was dialing Remington's number. A number that I had memorized long ago.

"Hello, Alexis."

"Hi, Remington. I don't have much time to talk but I said I would call you. So, what's up?"

This was classic behavior on my part. I had to act unbothered or play hard, as Remington would say. It was my defense mechanism to try to protect myself from hurt. Not that it had helped in this situation.

"Alexis, when are you coming home? Not Atlanta, but home. I would like to talk face to face."

"Oh you mean, when am I coming back to our house? I don't know."

"Why not? That's your home."

"Because I need to work through some shit and figure out my next move."

"Your next move? What does that…"

"I don't know what it means. I just know a lot has transpired and to think that things will be the same is ludicrous."

"I didn't say it would be the same, but I know we can work through this."

"How? What's your plan? How will I feel comfortable with you and your new baby?"

"It will take time but you can adjust. Hell, I even need to adjust."

"Wow, so I'm just expected to fall in line?"

"I didn't say that. I'm asking you to consider it and give it a try."

"You're asking a lot."

"Well, let me know when you'll be back in Atlanta so we can at least meet face to face. Preferably at our house so we can talk the way we need to talk."

"I'll be back in two days. I'll let you know when I decide to head over to the house and if you're not busy we can talk."

"I won't be busy and you know it."

"Bye, Remington."

"I love you, Alexis."

I didn't respond. I just hung up the phone. I was so emotionally torn. The stupid part of me did a happy dance because he said I love you. The logical part of me knew they were just words. Love hasn't made him do right by me and I'm not sure it will change things either.

The next couple of days with Mom were very relaxing. I tried not to think about Remington or our agreed upon meeting. I would be lying if I said I wasn't nervous. I was meeting with my ex fiancé to discuss our future. I'm not even really sure he was my ex fiancé since we hadn't officially broken it off. I shook my head to rid my thoughts of the whole situation.

When I arrived at Hartsfield Jackson International Airport, I'd never felt so relieved yet overwhelmed at the same time. I grabbed my luggage from baggage claim and headed to the designated waiting area for my Uber. I was headed to Brooklyn's house to get my car. While I was in the Uber, I text Remington to let him know I would be by the house in two hours if he was available.

I got my car from Brooklyn's and went to one of my favorite places to grab a bite to eat. I grabbed a seat on the patio at Le Petit Marche and enjoyed my food. Honestly, I was stalling. I didn't know how the conversation with Remington was going to play out so I needed some time to myself to think of every possible scenario and how I might want to respond. I finally headed home. It was on the drive home that I realized I never received a response from Remington. I decided to call instead of texting. I called his phone and it went straight to voicemail. I tried his business line and it just rang and rang. I called his personal phone again and it still went straight to voicemail. My feelings were so hurt. Here I was thinking he wanted to try to work something out and he was doing classic Remington behavior.

I pulled up to the house, took my luggage inside, and stood in the middle of the kitchen just looking at the representation of a life I had built. A life that had been built on a lie. I took the luggage into the master bedroom and didn't bother unpacking. I pulled a much smaller suitcase from the closet and put plenty of clothes in there. On the way out, I was going through the pile of mail left on the kitchen island. I didn't have much mail but I noticed Remington had lots of unopened mail. I wonder if that meant he hadn't been staying home. I tried to rid myself of those thoughts because I know it would only lead me to sadness. Shaking my head, I left and put my luggage in the car.

I decided that I needed a few more days to myself so I checked into the Marriott in downtown Atlanta. I checked my phone, hoping I would have a text from Remington but there was nothing. I sent a quick text to my mom to let her know I checked into the hotel safely. Before I realized what I was doing, I began searching for moving companies online. It was clear this relationship was over and I should look for a place to stay but in the meantime, I would look for a storage unit for my things.

I reached out to Sidney, my realtor, to see what I could do about getting off of the loan at the house and purchasing my own. I continued to search for a moving company and a reputable storage facility. When I finished searching for that I started browsing townhomes in various areas in metro Atlanta. Honestly, this was the most comfort I've had in a while. I found a few townhomes east of Atlanta and in Smyrna that caught my attention. I marked them and decided to focus on other things.

I had been back in Atlanta for two whole days and had yet to hear anything from Remington. I decided to move forward with my plan. I managed to secure a moving company and storage facility. Tomorrow, I was going to the house to get my things. I was up the next morning bright and early. The moving company would meet me at the house at 8:30 AM. By 7:45 I had already run, showered, and grabbed breakfast. I pulled up to the house around 8:15. I half expected Remington to be there but he wasn't. So, it confirmed that he wasn't staying at the house. Which could only mean that he was staying at his baby momma's house. My stomach was in knots. I don't know why this hurt so badly.

By 12:30 PM, we had all of my items packed and on the truck. The movers left because they were stopping to get lunch and we agreed to meet at the storage at two o'clock. I stood right in the middle of the walk-in closet and had an emotional meltdown. This was the worst feeling ever. I felt like I was walking away from everything I had worked for in this relationship. Hell, I felt like I was walking away from everything I had dreamt of and it hurt like shit. I needed a moment. I pulled my phone from my pocket and sent a text to a therapist that I found in the Therapy for Black Girls' directory.

Alexis: Hi, I'm Alexis. I'm looking to start therapy sessions. Are you accepting new patients?

I receive an instant reply.

Therapist: Hi, Alexis. Thanks for reaching out. I am taking new patients. Please go online and complete the survey and other documents. You'll be able to select a date for a session based on my availability.

Alexis: Thank you and I will do that before the end of the day.

Therapist: Thank you. I look forward to meeting you.

I needed to get my life back on track and therapy would be beneficial in that. At least, I hoped so. I pulled myself up and headed to my car to leave. Just as I was leaving, Reign called. We chatted briefly. I hadn't told her or Brooklyn that I moved all my stuff out. When I arrived at the storage unit I ended my conversation with Reign. The movers and I managed to get everything in place and we finished up by six o'clock. I was starving since I had only eaten breakfast. I didn't feel like showering, putting on clothes, and going somewhere so I ordered room service. This was the advantage of hotel living, but I missed cooking.

I settled in with my room service and pulled up the site for the therapist. I completed all the paperwork and scheduled an appointment for the following Monday. It was Thursday so I didn't have too many days to wait. Just as I pulled my journal out to begin writing, my phone dinged. It was a text from Remington.

Remington: Alexis, I'm so sorry. I had to take care of something.

Alexis: Whatever, Remington. You continue to show me what's important and it's definitely not me.

Remington: Alexis, don't act like that. Nikki had the baby. You know I wasn't going to miss that.

Alexis: Congratulations!

Remington: Thank you. Can we meet tomorrow? I'll be home then.

I didn't respond. I was too hurt to even think. She had the baby. I thought my feelings were hurt before but now it felt way worse than I could imagine. I pulled my journal out and decided to start writing. I wrote pages and pages of raw emotion. I wrote shit I didn't even know I felt or thought. After I finished writing, I cried. It seemed like I cried for hours. I'm not sure how long I cried. All I know is I woke Friday morning with a terrible headache and more than thirty text messages. Most of them were from Remington but I noticed I had two messages from Nikki. Why would she text me?

My better judgement was to not click on the message but curiosity won me over.

Nikki: Meet Remington Slayton, III or Tre as we like to call him.

The next text was an image of Nikki, the baby, and Remington at the hospital. My heart sunk. I didn't think I could get any lower in my heartache than what I was but I did. That was it for me. I blocked Nikki and Remington. It was best for me this way. I didn't bother reading Remington's messages. I just blocked both of their numbers and tried to focus on my tasks for the day. It was hard. I felt so empty and lonely.

Saturday morning, I tried to get back to some normalcy. I went for a long run and found a new brunch spot in East Atlanta. Afterwards, I decided to head to the outlets. Not that I needed any new clothes but retail therapy was good for me. I reached out to Brooke and Reign to see if we could get a girls' night in and of course they both agreed.

Just as I was heading out the door to go over to Reign's house, I got an email notification. It was from Remington.

From: Remington Slayton

To: Alexis Carter, Nicole

Subject: My Therapy Session

Wow… bet ya'll never thought you'd be getting a group email from me! But, here it goes…

First off, I want to apologize to both of you for bringing you into my mess and my insecurities. I went to a therapy session yesterday and spoke with my professional astrologer and here is what came out of those conversations:

When I sat down in front of the therapist, I explained to her what I had experienced and what I have gone through in the past several months. And of course, she has heard this story many times before and knew exactly what tools I could possibly use to move forward.

One of the first things she asked me was if I cared about both of you and I replied hesitantly, I believe I do. Yes, I care for Alexis and I care for Nicole. She also asked how long have I known each of you and I replied four years each with Nicole being a few months more.

I gave her the whole background on how I initially met Nicole online through a dating website and we were off and on still dealing with past relationships and never really hit it off although we were intimate. Of course, all that changed when we started working and spending more time together. I explained to her that I met Alexis when she reached out for graphic design services through my business. I had just gotten out of a horrible relationship with the mother of my ex coming on to me and attempting to be intimate with me. I discussed the terrible ending of that relationship and how I just rolled with the punches when it came to spending time with both of you.

We eventually began discussing some of the things that I can do to help everyone in the situation. Ironically, she had just finished a therapy session with two women and a man. She quickly explained that the couple had been married for twenty-two years and had the other woman in their relationship for the past eleven years. She further explained that this type of relationship was becoming more and more common. It was considered a V-type of relationship. Relationships of this caliber are on the far end of the spectrum. This type of relationship is the ultimate life experience and it requires complete honesty and transparency. She gave advice and tips on things I can do to move all of us forward… Alexis is definitely not going for that so I kind of blocked the idea out of my head. After the session ended, I had lots of thoughts on our relationship moving forward.

Now, I'm going to say how I feel. Alexis, I care about you. Nicole, I care about you. Here are some things I want to happen. Communicating openly about needs and wants in a relationship is what the therapist stressed. Alexis, I have felt like certain sexual activities in our relationship have been lacking. Now, this doesn't justify anything, it just gives an understanding of why certains things happened in certain situations. The therapist spoke of how bringing someone into the relationship with everyone consenting can increase passion, communication, quality of life, focus, health, and just all around living.

Nicole, I remembered a few years ago we toyed with the idea of bringing another person into an intimate setting with us but never acted on it. Now, this could be extreme even for me, but Alexis, what I would like to do is bring another person into our relationship. Not necessarily in the same room at the same time. Instead, I'd like it to be a situation where you know who I'm with, where we are, and what I'm doing. This would all be consensual and agreed upon. The other person will be Nicole. I trust Nicole. I know this is a lot but it is one of my ultimate desires before I die.

This email may fall on deaf ears which is fine and dandy with me. At least I have expressed some of the things that I have been thinking about with all honesty and truth. The therapist provided a list of benefits: builds trust, stronger communication, needs can be fulfilled, peace, opens our minds, healthier relationships, etc.

Whether it happens with two women that I trust and care for or not, this is something that I want to experience before I die. Rules can be set, boundaries can be implemented, and communication has to be authentic and true. This is exactly what you both wanted; open and honest communication. You will just get it in a non-traditional way. We will see where it goes… if it goes… hopefully, it will.

-R. Slayton

I sat in disbelief. The nerve of this crazy bastard. I was literally stunned. For the first time since this whole debacle began, I felt like I had made the best decision by leaving. I'm thankful I had gotten all of my stuff out of the house. This will be a good topic of discussion once I make it to Reign's house. I needed a few more minutes to gather my thoughts. I had already decided not to respond. I hope Nicole was smart enough not to respond but I'm sure she did. After a few minutes, I left my room and started on my way to Reign's house.

The girls and I spent the night laughing, drinking wine, planning my next move, and discussing the garbage ass email Remington sent. They were appalled at his audacity. While I felt relieved about my decision, it still hurt to watch someone you love turn into someone who you don't even recognize. Remington knew that damn email wasn't going to fly with me but he was arrogant enough to send it anyway. Bastard.

Sunday was a blur for me. I looked forward to my therapy session tomorrow. I also set an appointment with a real estate attorney. I needed to figure out how to get my name off the house and move on with my life. I would meet with Sidney that afternoon to look at a few townhomes for lease in my desired locations. It was definitely going to be a busy day so I took Sunday as my relaxation. I tried not to think about much at all.

My therapy session was scheduled for ten o'clock Monday morning. I was dressed and in the office parking lot by 9:30. I was so eager to speak with a therapist. I'm not sure if I was expecting a quick fix or not. I looked at my email and noticed another email from Remington. I'm sure he was wondering why I never responded to his "love triangle" email.

From: Remington Slayton

To: Alexis Carter

Subject: My Last Email

Hey, Alexis. I didn't really expect you to respond to my last email. I know it was a lot to take in and I know how you like to avoid situations you can't control. I also didn't expect for you to block my numbers. I have tried to call and text a few times but I know you didn't get them. Finally, I didn't expect for you to be moved totally out of the house. You have made it clear where you stand with this relationship.

Thanks for moving out so quickly. It makes it easier for my wife, Nicole, and my son to move in. Yes, we went to the courthouse and got married this morning. I hope you have retrieved all your items because you are no longer welcome in the Slayton's household. My attorney will be in contact soon.

-R. Slayton

To be continued…

CPSIA information can be obtained
at www.ICGtesting.com
Printed in the USA
BVHW092348060521
606654BV00004B/319